Nora Roberts is the *No...*
author of more than o...
novels. A born storyte...
of warmth, humour and poignancy that speaks
directly to her readers and has earned her almost
every award for excellence in her field. The
youngest of five children, Nora Roberts lives in
western Maryland. She has two sons.

Visit her website at www.noraroberts.com.

Also available by

Nora Roberts

Nora Roberts

Night Smoke

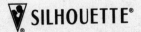

SILHOUETTE®

NIGHT SMOKE © Nora Roberts 1994

ISBN: 978 0 263 87721 2

026-0110

Silhouette Books' policy is to use papers that are
natural, renewable and recyclable products and made from
wood grown in sustainable forests. The logging and
manufacturing processes conform to the legal environmental
regulations of the country of origin.

Printed and bound in Spain
by Litografia Rosés S.A., Barcelona

For opposites who attract

Prologue

Fire. It cleansed. It destroyed. With its heat, lives could be saved. Or lives could be taken. It was one of the greatest discoveries of man, and one of his chief fears.

And one of his fascinations.

Mothers warned their children not to play with matches, not to touch the red glow of the stove. For no matter how pretty the flame, how seductive the warmth, fire against flesh burned.

In the hearth, it was romantic, cozy, cheerful, dancing and crackling, wafting scented smoke and flickering soft golden light. Old men dreamed by it. Lovers wooed by it.

In the campfire, it shot its sparks toward a starry sky, tempting wide-eyed children to roast their marshmallows into black goo while shivering over ghost stories.

There were dark, hopeless corners of the city where the homeless cupped their frozen hands over trash-can fires, their faces drawn and weary in the shadowy light, their minds too numb for dreams.

In the city of Urbana, there were many fires.

A carelessly dropped cigarette smoldering in a mattress. Faulty wiring, overlooked, or ignored by a corrupt inspector. A kerosene heater set too close to the drapes, oily rags tossed in a stuffy closet. A flash of lightning. An unattended candle.

All could cause destruction of property, loss of life. Ignorance, an accident, an act of God.

But there were other ways, more devious ways.

Once inside the building he took several short, shallow breaths. It was so simple, really. And so exciting. The power was in his hands now. He knew exactly what to do, and there was a thrill in doing it. Alone. In the dark.

It wouldn't be dark for long. The thought made him giggle as he climbed to the second floor. He would soon make the light.

Two cans of gasoline would be enough. With the first he splashed the old wooden floor, soaking it, leaving a trail as he moved from wall to wall, from room to room. Now and again he stopped, pulling stock from the racks, scattering matchbooks over the stream of flammables, adding fuel that would feed the flames and spread them.

The smell of the accelerant was sweet, an exotic perfume that heightened his senses. He wasn't panicked, he wasn't hurried as he climbed the winding metal stairs to the next floor. He was quiet, of course, for he wasn't a stupid man. But he knew the night watchman was bent over his magazines in another part of the building.

As he worked, he glanced up at the spider-like sprinklers in the ceiling. He'd already seen to those. There would be no hiss of water from the pipes as the flames rose, no warning buzz from smoke alarms.

This fire would burn, and burn, and burn, until the window glass exploded from the angry fists of heat. Paint would blister, metal would melt, rafters would fall, charred and flaming.

He wished…for a moment he wished he could stay, stand in the center of it all and watch the sleeping fire awaken, grumbling. He wanted to be there, to admire and absorb as it stirred, snapped, then stretched its hot, bright body. He wanted to hear its triumphant roar as it hungrily devoured everything in its path.

But he would be far away by then. Too far to see, to hear, to smell. He would have to imagine it.

With a sigh, he lit the first match, held the flame at eye level, admiring the infant spark, mesmerized by it. He was smiling, as proud as any expectant father, as he tossed the tiny fire into a dark pool of gas. He watched for a moment, only a moment, as the animal erupted into life, streaking along the trail he'd left for it.

He left quietly, hurrying now, into the frigid night. Soon his feet had picked up the rhythm of his racing heart.

Chapter 1

Annoyed, exhausted, Natalie stepped into her penthouse apartment. The dinner meeting with her marketing executives had run beyond midnight. She could have come home then, she reminded herself as she stepped out of her shoes. But no. Her office was en route from the restaurant to her apartment. She simply hadn't been able to resist stopping in for one more look at the new designs, one last check on the ads heralding the grand opening.

Both had needed work. And really, she'd only intended to make a few notes. Draft one or two memos.

So why was she stumbling toward the bedroom at 2:00 a.m.? she asked herself. The answer was easy. She was compulsive, obsessive. She was, Natalie thought, an idiot. Particularly since she had an eight-o'clock breakfast meeting with several of her East Coast sales reps.

No problem, she assured herself. No problem at all. Who needed sleep? Certainly not Natalie Fletcher, the thirty-two-year-old dynamo who was currently expanding Fletcher Industries into one more avenue of profit.

And there *would* be profit. She'd put all her skill and experience and creativity into building Lady's Choice from the ground up. Before profit, there would be the excitement of conception, birth, growth, those first pangs and pleasures of an infant company finding its own way.

Her infant company, she thought with tired satisfaction. Her baby. She would tend and teach and nurture—and, yes, when necessary, walk the floor at 2:00 a.m.

A glance in the mirror over the bureau told her that even a dynamo needed rest. Her cheeks had lost both their natural color as well as their cosmetic blush and her face looked entirely too fragile and pale. The simple twist that scooped her hair back and had started the evening looking sophisticated and chic now only seemed to emphasize the shadows that smudged her dark green eyes.

Because she was a woman who prided herself on her energy and stamina, she turned away from the reflection, blowing her honey-toned bangs out of her eyes and rotating her shoulders to ease the stiffness. In any case, sharks didn't sleep, she reminded herself. Even business sharks. But this one was very tempted to fall on the bed fully dressed.

That wouldn't do, she thought, and shrugged out of her coat. Organization and control were every bit as important in business as a good head for figures. Ingrained habit had her walking to the closet, and she was draping the velvet wrap on a padded hanger when the phone rang.

Let the machine get it, she ordered herself, but by the second ring she was snatching up the receiver.

"Hello?"

"Ms. Fletcher?"

"Yes?" The receiver clanged against the emeralds at her ear. She was reaching up to remove the earring when the panic in the voice stopped her.

"It's Jim Banks, Ms. Fletcher. The night watch-man over at the south side warehouse. We've got trouble here."

"Trouble? Did someone break in?"

"It's fire. Holy God, Ms. Fletcher, the whole place is going up."

"Fire?" She brought her other hand to the re-ceiver, as if it might leap from her ear. "At the warehouse? Was anyone in the building? Is any-one in there?"

"No, ma'am, there was just me." His voice shook, cracked. "I was downstairs in the coffee room when I heard an explosion. Must've been a bomb or something, I don't know. I called the fire department."

She could hear other sounds now, sirens, shouts. "Are you hurt?"

"No, I got out. I got out. Mother of God, Ms. Fletcher, it's terrible. It's just terrible."

"I'm on my way."

It took Natalie fifteen minutes to make the trip from her plush west-side neighborhood to the dingy south side, with its warehouses and facto-ries. But she saw the fire, heard it before she pulled up behind the string of engines. Men with their faces smeared with soot manned hoses, wielded axes. Smoke and flame belched from shattered windows and spewed through gaps in the ruined roof. The heat was enormous. Even at this distance it shot out, slapping her face while the icy February wind swirled at her back.

Everything. She knew everything inside the building was lost.

"Ms. Fletcher?"

Struggling against horror and fascination, she turned and looked at a round middle-aged man in a gray uniform.

"I'm Jim Banks."

"Oh, yes." She reached out automatically to take his hand. It was freezing, and as shaky as his voice. "You're all right? Are you sure?"

"Yes, ma'am. It's an awful thing."

They watched the fire and those who fought it for a moment, in silence. "The smoke alarms?"

"I didn't hear anything. Not until the explosion. I started to head upstairs, and I saw the fire. It was everywhere." He rubbed a hand over his mouth. Never in his life had he seen anything like it. Never in his life did he want to see its like again. "Just everywhere. I got out and called the fire department from my truck."

"You did the right thing. Do you know who's in charge here?"

"No, Ms. Fletcher, I don't. These guys work fast, and they don't spend a lot of time talking."

"All right. Why don't you go home now, Jim? I'll deal with this. If they need to talk to you, I have your beeper number, and they can call."

"Nothing much to do." He looked down at the ground and shook his head. "I'm mighty sorry, Ms. Fletcher."

"So am I. I appreciate you calling me."

"Thought I should." He gave one last glance at the building, seemed to shudder, then trudged off to his truck.

Natalie stood where she was, and waited.

A crowd had gathered by the time Ry got to the scene. A fire drew crowds, he knew, like a good fistfight or a flashy juggler. People even took sides—and a great many of them rooted for the fire.

He stepped out of his car, a lean, broad-shouldered man with tired eyes the color of the smoke stinging the winter sky. His narrow, bony face was set, impassive. The lights flashing around him shadowed, then highlighted, the hollows and planes, the shallow cleft in his chin that women loved and he found a small nuisance.

He set his boots on the sodden ground and stepped into them with a grace and economy of motion that came from years of training. Though flames still licked and sparked, his experienced eye told him that the men had contained and nearly suppressed it.

Soon it would be time for him to go to work.

Automatically he put on the black protective jacket, covering his flannel shirt and his jeans down past the hips. He combed one hand through his unruly hair, hair that was a deep, dark brown and showed hints of fire in sunlight. He set his dented, smoke-stained hat on his head, lit a cigarette, then tugged on protective gloves.

And while he performed these habitual acts, he scanned the scene. A man in his position needed to keep an open mind about fire. He would take an overview of the scene, the weather, note the wind direction, talk to the fire fighters. There would be all manner of routine and scientific tests to run.

But first, he would trust his eyes, and his nose.

The warehouse was most probably a loss, but it was no longer his job to save it. His job was to find the whys and the hows.

He exhaled smoke and studied the crowd.

He knew the night watchman had called in the alarm. The man would have to be interviewed. Ry looked over the faces, one by one. Excitement was normal. He saw it in the eyes of the young man who watched the destruction, dazzled. And shock, in the slack-jawed woman who huddled against him. Horror, admiration, relief that the fire hadn't touched them or theirs. He saw that, as well.

Then his gaze fell on the blonde.

She stood apart from the rest, staring straight ahead while the light wind teased her honey blond hair out of its fancy twist. Expensive shoes, Ry noted, of supple midnight leather, as out of place in this part of town as her velvet coat and her fancy face.

A hell of a face, he thought idly, lifting the cigarette to his lips again. A pale oval that belonged on a cameo. Eyes... He couldn't make out their color, but they were dark. No excitement there, he mused. No horror, no shock. Anger, maybe. Just a touch of it. She was either a woman of little emotion, or one who knew how to control it.

A hothouse rose, he decided. And just what was she doing so far out of her milieu at nearly four o'clock in the morning?

"Hey, Inspector." Grimy and wet, Lieutenant Holden trudged over to bum a cigarette. "Chalk up another one for the Fighting Twenty-second."

Ry knew Holden, and was already holding the pack out. "Looks like you killed another one."

"This was a bitch." Cupping his hands against the wind, Holden lit up. "Fully involved by the time we got here. Call came in from the night watchman at 1:40. Second and third floors took most of it, but the equipment on one's pretty well gone, too. You'll probably find your point of origin on the second."

"Yeah?" Though the fire was winding down, Ry knew Holden wasn't just shooting the breeze.

"Found some streamers going up the steps at the east end. Probably started the fire with them, but not all the material went up. Ladies' lingerie."

"Hmmm?"

"Ladies' lingerie," Holden said with a grin. "That's what they were warehousing. Lots of nighties and undies. You've got a nice stream of underwear and matchbooks that didn't go up." He slapped Ry on the shoulder. "Have fun. Hey, probie!" he shouted to one of the probationary firefighters. "You going to hold that hose or play with it? Got to watch 'em every minute, Ry."

"Don't I know it…"

Out of the corner of his eye, Ry watched his hothouse flower pick her way toward a fire engine. He and Holden separated.

"Isn't there anything you can tell me?" Natalie asked an exhausted firefighter. "How did it start?"

"Lady, I just put them out." He sat on a running board, no longer interested in the smoldering wreck of the warehouse. "You want answers?" He jerked his thumb in Ry's direction. "Ask the inspector."

"Civilians don't belong at fire scenes," Ry said from behind her. When she turned to look at him, he saw that her eyes were green, a deep jade green.

"It's my fire scene." Her voice was cool, like the wind that teased her hair, with a faint drawl that made him think of cowboys and schoolmarms. "My warehouse," she continued. "My problem."

"Is that so?" Ry took another survey. She was cold. He knew from experience that there was no place colder than a fire scene in winter. But her spine was straight, and that delicate chin lifted. "And that would make you…?"

"Natalie Fletcher. I own the building, and everything in it. And I'd like some answers." She cocked one elegantly arched brow. "And that would make you—?"

"Piasecki. Arson investigator."

"Arson?" Shock had her gaping before she snapped back into control. "You think this was arson."

"It's my job to find out." He glanced down, nearly sneered. "You're going to ruin those shoes, Miz Fletcher."

"My shoes are the least of my—" She broke off when he took her arm and started to steer her away. "What are you doing?"

"You're in the way. That would be your car, wouldn't it?" He nodded toward a shiny new Mercedes convertible.

"Yes, but—"

"Get in it."

"I will not get in it." She tried to shake him off and discovered she would have needed a crowbar. "Will you let go of me?"

She smelled a hell of a lot better than smoke and sodden debris. Ry took a deep gulp of her, then tried for diplomacy. It was something, he was proud to admit, that had never been his strong suit.

"Look, you're cold. What's the point in standing out in the wind?"

She stiffened, against both him and the wind. "The point is, that's my building. What's left of it."

"Fine." They'd do it her way, since it suited him. But he placed her between the car and his body to shelter her from the worst of the cold. "It's kind of late at night to be checking your inventory, isn't it?"

"It is." She stuck her hands in her pockets, trying fruitlessly to warm them. "I drove out after the night watchman called me."

"And that would have been…"

"I don't know. Around two."

"Around two," he repeated, and let his gaze skim over her again. There was a snazzy dinner suit under the velvet, he noted. The material looked soft, expensive, and it was the same color as her eyes. "Pretty fancy outfit for a fire."

"I had a late meeting and didn't think to change into more appropriate clothes before I came." Idiot, she thought, and looked back grimly at what was left of her property. "Is there a point to this?"

"Your meeting ran until two?"

"No, it broke up about midnight."

"How come you're still dressed?"

"What?"

"How come you're still dressed?" He took out another cigarette, lit it. "Late date?"

"No, I went by my office to do some paperwork.

I'd barely gotten home when Jim Banks, the night watchman, called me."

"Then you were alone from midnight until two?"

"Yes, I—" Her eyes cut back to his, narrowed. "Do you think I'm responsible for this? Is that what you're getting at here—? What the hell was your name?"

"Piasecki," he said, and smiled. "Ryan Piasecki. And I don't think anything yet, Miz Fletcher. I'm just separating the details."

Her eyes were no longer cool, controlled. They had flared to flash point. "Then I'll give you some more. The building and its contents are fully insured. I'm with United Security."

"What kind of business are you in?"

"I'm Fletcher Industries, Inspector Piasecki. You may have heard of it."

He had, most certainly. Real estate, mining, shipping. The conglomerate owned considerable property, including several holdings in Urbana. But there were reasons that big companies, as well as small ones, resorted to arson.

"You run Fletcher Industries?"

"I oversee several of its interests. Including this one." Most particularly this one, she thought. This one was her baby. "We're opening several speciality boutiques countrywide in the spring, in addition to a catalog service. A large portion of my inventory was in that building."

"What sort of inventory?"

Now she smiled. "Lingerie, inspector. Bras, panties, negligees. Silks, satins, lace. You might be familiar with the concept."

"Enough to appreciate it." She was shivering now, obviously struggling to keep her teeth from chattering. He imagined her feet would be blocks of ice in those thin, pricey shoes. "Look, you're freezing out here. Get in the car. Go home. We'll be in touch."

"I want to know what happened to my building. What's left of my stock."

"Your building burned down, Miz Fletcher. And it's unlikely there's anything left of your stock that would raise a man's blood pressure." He opened the car door. "I've got a job to do. And I'd advise you to call your insurance agent."

"You've got a real knack for soothing the victims, don't you, Piasecki?"

"No, can't say that I do." He took a notebook and pencil stub from his shirt pocket. "Give me your address and phone number. Home and office."

Natalie took a deep breath, then let it out slowly, before she gave him the information he wanted. "You know," she added. "I've always had a soft spot for public servants. My brother's a cop in Denver."

"That so?"

"Yes, that's so." She slid into the car. "You've managed, in one short meeting, to change my mind." She slammed the door, sorry she didn't do it quickly enough to catch his fingers. With one last glance at the ruined building, she drove away.

Ry watched her taillights disappear and added another note to his book. Great legs. Not that he'd forget, he mused as he turned away. But a good inspector wrote everything down.

Natalie forced herself to sleep for two hours, then rose and took a stinging-cold shower. Wrapped in her robe, she called her assistant and arranged to have her morning appointments canceled or shifted. With her first cup of coffee, she phoned her parents in Colorado. She was on cup number two by the time she had given them all the details she knew, soothed their concern and listened to their advice.

With cup number three, she contacted her insurance agent and arranged to meet him at the site. After downing aspirin with the remains of that cup, she dressed for what promised to be a very long day.

She was nearly out of the door when the phone stopped her.

"You have a machine," she reminded herself, even as she darted back to answer it. "Hello?"

"Nat, it's Deborah. I just heard."

"Oh." Rubbing the back of her neck, Natalie sat on the arm of a chair. Deborah O'Roarke Guthrie was a double pleasure, both friend and family. "I guess it's hit the news already."

There was a slight hesitation. "I'm sorry, Natalie, really sorry. How bad is it?"

"I'm not sure. Last night it looked about as bad as it gets. But I'm going out now, meeting my insurance agent. Who knows, we may salvage something."

"Would you like me to come with you? I can reschedule my morning."

Natalie smiled. Deborah would do just that. As if she didn't have enough on her plate with her husband, her baby, her job as assistant district attorney.

"No, but thanks for asking. I'll let you know something when I know something."

"Come to dinner tonight. You can relax, soak up some sympathy."

"I'd like that."

"If there's anything else I can do, just tell me."

"Actually, you could call Denver. Keep your sister and my brother from riding east to the rescue."

"I'll do that."

"Oh, one more thing." Natalie rose, checked the contents of her briefcase as she spoke. "What do you know about an Inspector Piasecki? Ryan Piasecki?"

"Piasecki?" There was a slight pause as Deborah flipped through her mental files. Natalie could all but see the process. "Arson squad. He's the best in the city."

"He would be," Natalie muttered.

"Is arson suspected?" Deborah said carefully.

"I don't know. I just know he was there, he was rude, and he wouldn't tell me anything."

"It takes time to determine the cause of a fire, Natalie. I can put some pressure on, if you want me to."

It was tempting, just for the imagined pleasure of seeing Piasecki scramble. "No thanks. Not yet, anyway. I'll see you later."

"Seven o'clock," Deborah insisted.

"I'll be there. Thanks." Natalie hung up and grabbed her coat. With luck, she'd beat the insurance agent to the site by a good thirty minutes.

Luck was with her—in that area, anyway. When Natalie pulled up behind the fire-department barricade, she discovered she was going to need a great deal more than luck to win this battle.

It looked worse, incredibly worse, than it had the night before.

It was a small building, only three floors. The cinder-block outer walls had held, and now stood blackened and streaked with soot, still dripping with water from the hoses. The ground was littered with charred and sodden wood, broken glass, twisted metal. The air stank of smoke.

Miserable, she ducked under the yellow tape for a closer look.

"What the hell do you think you're doing?"

She jolted, then shaded her eyes from the sun to see more clearly. She should have known, Natalie thought, when she saw Ry making his way toward her through the wreckage.

"Didn't you see the sign?" he demanded.

"Of course I saw it. This is my property, Inspector. The insurance adjuster is meeting me here shortly. I believe I'm within my rights in inspecting the damage."

He gave her one disgusted look. "Don't you have any other kind of shoes?"

"I beg your pardon?"

"Stay here." Muttering to himself, he stalked to his car, came back with a pair of oversize fireman's boots. "Put these on."

"But—"

He took her arm, throwing her off balance. "Put those ridiculous shoes into the boots. Otherwise you're going to hurt yourself."

"Fine." She stepped into them, feeling absurd.

The tops of the boots covered her legs almost to the knee. The navy suit and matching wool coat she wore were runway-model smart. A trio of gold chains draped around her neck added flash.

"Nice look," he commented. "Now, let's get something straight. I need to preserve this scene, and that means you don't touch anything." He said it even though his authority to keep her out was debatable, and he'd already found a great deal of what he'd been looking for.

"I have no intention of—"

"That's what they all say."

She drew herself up. "Tell me, Inspector, do you work alone because you prefer it, or because no one can stand to be around you for longer than five minutes?"

"Both." He smiled then. The change of expression was dazzling, charming—and suspicious. She wasn't sure, but she thought the faintest of dimples winked beside his mouth. "What are you doing clunking around a fire scene in a five-hundred-dollar suit?"

"I…" Wary of the smile, she tugged her coat closed. "I have meetings all afternoon. I won't have time to change."

"Executives." He kept his hand on her arm as he turned. "Come on, then. Be careful where you go—the site's not totally safe, but you can take a look at what she left you. I've still got work to do."

He led her in through the mangled doorway. The ceiling was a yawning pit between floors. What had fallen, or had been knocked through, lay in filthy layers of sodden ash and alligatored wood. She shivered once at the sight of the twisted mass of burned mannequins that lay sprawled and broken.

"They didn't suffer," Ry assured her, and her eyes flashed back to his.

"I'm sure you can view this as a joke, but—"

"Fire's never a joke. Watch your step."

She saw where he'd been working, near the base of a broken inner wall. There was a small wire screen in a wooden frame, a shovel that looked like a child's toy, a few mason jars, a crowbar, a yardstick. While she watched, Ry pried off a scored section of baseboard.

"What are you doing?"

"My job."

She set her teeth. "Are we on the same side here?"

He glanced up. "Maybe." With a putty knife, he began to scrape at residue. He sniffed, he grunted and, when he was satisfied, placed it in a jar. "Do you know what oxidation is, Ms. Fletcher?"

She frowned, shifted. "More or less."

"The chemical union of a substance with oxygen. It can be slow, like paint drying, or fast. Heat and light. A fire's fast. And some things help it move faster." He continued to scrape, then looked up again, held out the knife. "Take a whiff."

Dubious, she stepped forward and sniffed.

"What do you smell?"

"Smoke, wet…I don't know."

He placed the residue in the jar. "Gasoline," he

said, watching her face. "See, a liquid seeks its level, goes into cracks in the floor, into dead-air corners, flows under baseboard. If it gets caught under there, it doesn't burn. You see the place I cleared out here?"

She moistened her lips, studied the floor he had shoveled or swept clear of debris. There was a black stain, like a shadow burned into the wood. "Yes?"

"The charred-blob pattern. It's like a map. I keep at this, layer by layer, and I'll be able to tell what happened, before, during."

"You're telling me someone poured gas in here and lit a match?"

He said nothing, only scooted forward a bit to pick up a scrap of burned cloth. "Silk," he said with a rub of his fingertips. "Too bad." He placed the scrap in what looked like a flour tin. "Sometimes a torch will lay out streamers, give the fire more of an appetite. They don't always burn." He picked up an almost perfectly preserved cup from a lacy bra. Amused, his eyes met Natalie's over it. "Funny what resists, isn't it?"

She was cold again, but not from the wind. It was from within, and it was rage. "If this fire was deliberately set, I want to know."

Interested in the change in her eyes, he sat back on his haunches. His black fireman's coat was unhooked, revealing jeans, worn white at the knees, and a flannel shirt. He hadn't left the scene since his arrival.

"You'll get my report." He rose then. "Draw me a picture. What did this place look like twenty-four hours ago?"

She closed her eyes for a moment, but it didn't help. She could still smell the destruction.

"It was three stories, about two thousand square feet. Iron balconies and interior steps. Seamstresses worked on the third floor. All of our merchandise is handmade."

"Classy."

"Yes, that's the idea. We have another plant in this district where most of the sewing is done. The twelve machines upstairs were just for finish work. There was a small coffee room to the left, rest rooms… On the second, the floor was made of linoleum, rather than wood. We stored the stock there. I kept a small office up there, as well, though I do most of my work uptown. The area down here was for inspecting, packaging and shipping. We were to begin fulfilling our spring orders in three weeks."

She turned, not quite sure where she intended to go, and stumbled over debris. Ry's quick grab saved her from a nasty spill.

"Hold on," he murmured.

Shaken, she leaned back against him for a moment. There was strength there, if not sympathy. At the moment, she preferred it that way. "We employed over seventy people in this plant alone. People who are out of work until I can sort this out." She whirled back. He gripped her arms to keep her steady. "And it was deliberate."

Control, he thought. Well, she didn't have it now. She was as volatile as a lit match. "I haven't finished my investigation."

"It was deliberate," she repeated. "And you're thinking I could have done it. That I came in here in the middle of the night with a can of gasoline."

Her face was close to his. Funny, he thought, he hadn't noticed how tall she was in those fancy ankle-breaking shoes. "It's a little hard to picture."

"Hired someone, then?" she tossed out. "Hired someone to burn down the building, even though there was a man in it? But what's one security guard against a nice fat insurance check?"

He was silent for a moment, his eyes locked on hers. "You tell me."

Infuriated, she wrenched away from him. "No, Inspector, you're going to have to tell me. And whether you like it or not, I'm going to be on you like a shadow through every step of the investigation. Every step," she repeated. "Until I have all the answers."

She strode out of the building, dignified despite the awkward boots. Her temper was barely under control when she saw the car pull up beside hers. Recognizing it, she sighed, made her way to the tape barrier and under it.

"Donald." She held out her hands. "Oh, Donald, what a mess…"

Gripping her hands, he looked beyond her to the building. For a moment he just stood there, holding her hands, shaking his head. "How could this have happened? The wiring? We had the wiring checked two months ago."

"I know. I'm so sorry. All your work." Two years of his life, she thought, and hers. Up in smoke.

"Everything?" There was a faint tremor in his voice, in his hand as it gripped hers. "Is it all gone?"

"I'm afraid it is. We have other inventory, Donald. This isn't going to whip us."

"You're tougher than me, Nat." After a last quick squeeze he released her hands. "This was my biggest shot. You're the CEO, but I feel like I was captain. And my ship just sank."

Natalie's heart went out to him. It wasn't simply business with Donald Hawthorne, she thought, any more than it was simply business with her. This new company was a dream, a fresh excitement, and a chance for both of them to try something completely different.

No, not just to try, she reminded herself. To succeed.

"We're going to have to work our butts off for the next three weeks."

He turned back, a small smile curving his lips. "Do you really think we can pull it off, after this, on schedule?"

"Yes, I do." Determination hardened her lips. "It's a delay, that's all. So we shuffle things around. We'll certainly have to postpone the audit."

"I can't even think of that now." He stopped, blinked. "Jesus, Nat, the files, the records."

"I don't think we're going to salvage any of the paperwork that was in the warehouse." She looked back toward her building. "It's going to make things more complicated, add some work hours, but we'll put it back together."

"But how can we manage the audit when—"

"It goes on the back burner until we're up and running. We'll talk about it back at the office. As soon as I meet the insurance agent, get the ball rolling, I'm heading back in." Already her mind was working out the details, the steps and stages. "We'll put on some double shifts, order new material, pull in some inventory from Chicago and Atlanta. We'll make it work, Donald. Lady's Choice is going to open in April, come hell or high water."

His smile flashed into a grin. "If anybody can make it work, you can."

"*We* can," she told him. "Now I need you to get back uptown, start making calls." PR, she knew, was his strong suit. He was overly impulsive perhaps, but she needed the action-oriented with her now. "You get Melvin and Deirdre hopping, Donald. Bribe or threaten distributors, plead with the union, soothe the clients. That's what you do best."

"I'm on it. You can count on me."

"I know I can. I'll be in the office soon to crack the whip."

* * *

Boyfriend? Ry wondered as he watched the two embrace. The tall, polished executive with the pretty face and shiny shoes looked to be her type.

As a matter of course, he noted down the license number of the Lincoln beside Natalie's car, then went back to work.

Chapter 2

"She's going to be here any minute." Assistant District Attorney Deborah O'Roarke Guthrie put fisted hands on her hips. "I want the whole story, Gage, before Natalie gets here."

Gage added another log to the fire before he turned to his wife. She'd changed out of her business suit into soft wool slacks and a cashmere sweater of midnight blue. Her ebony hair fell loose, nearly to her shoulders.

"You're beautiful, Deborah. I don't tell you that often enough."

She lifted a brow. Oh, he was a smooth operator, and charming. And clever. But so was she. "No evasions, Gage. You've managed to avoid telling me everything you know so far, but—"

"You were in court all day," he reminded her. "I was in meetings."

"That's beside the point. I'm here now."

"You certainly are." He walked to her, slipped his arms through hers and circled her waist. His lips curved as they lowered to hers. "Hello."

More than two years of marriage hadn't diluted her response to him. Her mouth softened, parted, but then she remembered herself and stepped back. "No, you don't. Consider yourself under oath and in the witness chair, Guthrie. Spill it. I know you were there."

"I was there." Annoyance flickered in his eyes before he crossed over to pour mineral water for Deborah. Yes, he'd been there, he thought. Too late.

He had his own way of combating the dark side of Urbana. The gift—or the curse—he'd been left with after surviving what should have been a fatal shooting gave him an edge. He'd been a cop too long to close his eyes to injustice. Now, with the odd twist fate had dealt him, he fought crime his own way, with his own special talent.

Deborah watched him stare down at his hand, flex it. It was an old habit, one that told her he was thinking of how he could make it, make himself fade to nothing.

And when he did, he was Nemesis, a shadow that haunted the streets of Urbana, a shadow that had slipped into her life, and her heart as real and as dear to her as the man who stood before her.

"I was there," he repeated, and poured a glass of wine for himself. "But too late to do anything. I didn't beat the first engine company by more than five minutes."

"You can't always be first on the scene, Gage," Deborah murmured. "Even Nemesis isn't omnipotent."

"No." He handed her the glass. "The point is, I didn't see who started the fire. If indeed it was arson."

"Which you believe it was."

He smiled again. "I have a suspicious mind."

"So do I." She tapped her glass against his. "I wish there was something I could do for Natalie. She's worked so hard to get this new company off the ground."

"You're doing something," Gage told her. "You're here. And she'll fight back."

"That's one thing you can count on." She tilted her head. "I don't suppose anyone saw you around the warehouse last night."

Now he grinned. "What do you think?"

She blew out a breath. "I think I'll never quite get used to it." When the doorbell sounded, Deborah set her glass aside. "I'll get it." She hurried to the door, then opened her arms to Natalie. "I'm so glad you could come."

"I wouldn't miss one of Frank's meals for anything." Determined to be cheerful, Natalie kissed Deborah, then linked arms with her as they walked back into the sitting room. She offered her host a brilliant smile. "Hello, gorgeous."

She kissed Gage, as well, accepted the drink he offered and a seat by the fire. She sighed once. A beautiful house, a beautiful couple, so incredibly in love. Natalie told herself if she were inclined toward domesticity, she might be envious.

"How are you coping?" Deborah asked her.

"Well, I love a challenge, and this is a big one. The bottom line is, Lady's Choice will have its grand opening, nationwide, in three weeks."

"I was under the impression that you lost quite a bit of merchandise," Gage commented. Cloaked by the shadow of his gift, he'd watched her arrive at the scene the night before. "As well as the building."

"There are other buildings."

In fact, she had already arranged to purchase another warehouse. It would, even after the insurance payoff, put a dent in the estimated profits for the year. But they would make it up, Natalie thought. She would see to that.

"We're going to be working overtime for a while to make up some of the losses. And I can pull some stock in from other locations. Urbana's our flagship store. I intend for it to go off with a bang."

She sipped her wine, running the stages through her mind. "I've got Donald with a phone glued to his ear. With his background in public relations, he's the best qualified to beg and borrow. Melvin's already flown out on a four-city jaunt to swing through the other plants and stores. He'll work some of his wizardry in figuring who can spare what merchandise. And Deirdre's working on the figures. I've talked to the union leaders, and some of the laborers. I intend to be back in full production within forty-eight hours."

Gage toasted her. "If anyone can do it…" He was a businessman himself. Among other things.

And knew exactly how much work, how much risk and how much sweat Natalie would face. "Is there anything new on the fire itself?"

"Not specifically." Frowning, Natalie glanced into the cheerful flames in the hearth. So harmless, she thought, so attractive. "I've talked with the investigator a couple of times. He implies, he interrogates, and, by God, he irritates. But he doesn't commit."

"Ryan Piasecki," Deborah stated, and it was her turn to smile. "I stole a few minutes today to do some checking on him. I thought you'd be interested."

"Bless you." Natalie leaned forward. "So, what's the story?"

"He's been with the department for fifteen years. Fought fires for ten, and worked his way up to lieutenant. A couple of smears in his file."

Natalie's lips curved smugly. "Oh, really?"

"Apparently he belted a city councilman at a fire scene. Broke his jaw."

"Violent tendencies," Natalie muttered. "I knew it."

"It was what they call a class C fire," Deborah continued. "In a chemical plant. Piasecki was with engine company 18, and they were the first to respond. There was no backup. Economic cutbacks," she added as Natalie's brows knit. "Number 18 lost three men in that fire, and two more were critically injured. The councilman showed up with the press in tow and began to pontificate on our system at work. He'd spearheaded the cutbacks."

Damn it. Natalie blew out a breath. "I guess I'd have belted him, too."

"There was another disciplinary action when he stormed into the mayor's office with a bagful of fire-site salvage and dumped it on the desk. It was from a low-rent apartment building on the east side, that had just passed inspection—even though the wiring was bad, the furnace faulty. No smoke alarms. Broken fire escapes. Twenty people died."

"I wanted you to tell me that my instincts were on target," Natalie muttered. "That I had a good reason for detesting him."

"Sorry." Deborah had developed a soft spot for men who fought crime and corruption in untraditional manners. She shot Gage a look that warmed them both.

"Well." Natalie sighed. "What else do you have on him?"

"He moved to the arson squad about five years

ago. He has a reputation for being abrasive, aggressive and annoying."

"That's better."

"And for having the nose of a bloodhound, the eyes of a hawk, and the tenacity of a pit bull. He keeps digging and digging until he finds the answers. I've never had to use him in court, but I asked around. You can't shake him on the stand. He's smart. He writes everything down. Everything. And he remembers it. He's thirty-six, divorced. He's a team player who prefers to work alone."

"I suppose it should make me feel better, knowing I'm in competent hands." Natalie moved her shoulders restlessly. "But it doesn't. I appreciate the profile."

"No problem," Deborah began, then broke off when the sound of crying came through the baby monitor beside her. "Sounds like the boss is awake. No, I'll go," she said when Gage got to his feet. "She just wants company."

"Am I going to get a peek?" Natalie asked.

"Sure, come on."

"I'll tell Frank to hold dinner until you're done." With a frown in his eyes, Gage watched Natalie head upstairs with his wife.

"You know," Natalie said as they started up to the nursery, "you look fabulous. I don't see how you manage it all. A demanding career, a dynamic husband and all the social obligations that go with him, and the adorable Adrianna."

"I could tell you it's all a matter of time management and prioritizing." With a grin, Deborah opened the door of the nursery. "But what it really comes down to is passion. For the job, for Gage, for our Addy. There's nothing you can't have, if you're passionate about it."

The nursery was a symphony of color. Murals on the ceiling told stories of princesses and magic horses. Primary tones brightened the walls and bled into rainbows. With her hands gripped on the rail of her Jenny Lind crib, legs wobbling, ten-month-old Addy pouted, oblivious of the ambiance.

"Oh, sweetie." Deborah reached down, picked her up to nuzzle. "Here you are, all wet and lonely."

The pout transformed into a beaming, satisfied smile. "Mama."

Natalie watched while Deborah laid Addy on the changing table.

"She's prettier every time I see her." Gently she

brushed at the dark thatch of hair on the baby's head. Pleased with the attention, Addy kicked her feet and began to babble.

"We're thinking about having another."

"Another?" Natalie blinked into Deborah's glowing face. "Already?"

"Well, it's still in the what-if stage. But we'd really like to have three." She pressed a kiss to the soft curve of Addy's neck, chuckling when she tugged on her hair. "I just love being a mother."

"It shows. Can I?" Once the fresh diaper was in place, Natalie lifted the baby.

There was envy, she discovered, for this small miracle who curved so perfectly into her arms.

Two days later, Natalie was at her desk, a headache drumming behind her eyes. She didn't mind it. The incessant throbbing pushed her forward.

"If the mechanic can't repair the machines, get new ones. I want every seamstress on-line. No, tomorrow afternoon won't do." She tapped a pen on the edge of her desk, shifted the phone from ear to ear. "Today. I'll be in myself by one to check on the new stock. I know it's a madhouse. Let's keep it that way."

She hung up and looked at her three associates. "Donald?"

He skimmed a hand over his burnished hair. "The first ad runs in the *Times* on Saturday. Full-page, three-color. The ad, with necessary variations, will be running in the other cities simultaneously."

"The changes I wanted?"

"Implemented. Catalogs shipped today. They look fabulous."

"Yes, they do." Pleased, Natalie glanced down at the glossy catalog on her desk. "Melvin?"

As was his habit, Melvin Glasky slipped off his rimless glasses, polishing them as he spoke. He was in his mid-fifties, addicted to bow ties and golf. He was thin of frame and pink of cheek, and sported a salt-and-pepper toupee that he naively believed was his little secret.

"Atlanta looks the best, though Chicago and L.A. are gearing up." He gestured to the report on her desk. "I worked out deals with each location for inventory transfers. Not everybody was happy about it." His lenses glinted like diamonds when he set them back on his nose. "The store manager in Chicago defended her stock like a mama bear. She didn't want to give up one brassiere."

Natalie's lips twitched at his drawling pronunciation. "So?"

"So I blamed it on you."

Natalie leaned back in her chair and chuckled. "Of course you did."

"I told her that you wanted twice what you'd told me you needed. Which gave me negotiating room. She figured you should filch from catalog. I agreed." His eyes twinkled. "Then I told her how you considered catalog sacred. Wouldn't touch one pair of panties, because you wanted all catalog orders fulfilled within ten days of order. You're inflexible."

Her lips twitched again. In the eighteen months they'd worked together on this project, she'd come to adore Melvin. "I certainly am."

"So I told her how I'd take the heat, and half of what you ordered."

"You'd have made a hell of a politician, Melvin."

"What do you think I am? In any case, you've got about fifty percent of your inventory back for the flagship store."

"I owe you. Deirdre?"

"I've run the projected increases in payroll and material expenses." Deirdre Marks tossed her flyaway ginger braid behind her shoulder. Her slightly flattened tones were pure Midwest, and her mind was as quick and controlled as a high-tech computer. "Also the outlay for the new site and equipment. With the incentive bonuses you authorized, we'll be in the red. I've done graphs—"

"I've seen them." Mulling over her options, Natalie rubbed the back of her neck. "The insurance money, when it comes through, will offset that somewhat. I'm willing to risk my investment, and add to it, to see that this works."

"From a straight financial standpoint," Deirdre continued, "any return looks dim. At least in the foreseeable future. First-year sales alone would have to be in excess of…" She shrugged her narrow shoulders at Natalie's stubborn expression. "You have the figures."

"Yes, and I appreciate the extra work. The files at the south side warehouse were destroyed. Fortunately, I'd had Maureen make copies of the bulk of them." She rubbed her eyes, caught herself and folded her hands. "I'm very aware that the majority of new business ventures fold within the first year. This isn't going to be one of them. I'm not looking for short-term profits, but for long-term success. I intend for Lady's Choice to be at the top on retail and direct sales within ten years. So I'm certainly not going to take a step back at the first real obstacle."

She flicked a finger over a button when her buzzer sounded. "Yes, Maureen?"

"Inspector Piasecki would like to see you, Ms. Fletcher. He doesn't have an appointment."

Automatically Natalie scanned her desk calendar. She could spare Piasecki fifteen minutes and still make it to the new warehouse. "We'll have to finish this later," she said with a glance at her associates. "Show him in, Maureen."

Ry preferred meeting friends or foes on their own turf. He hadn't yet decided which category Natalie Fletcher fell into. He had, however, decided to swing by her office to get a firsthand look at that part of her operation.

He couldn't say he was disappointed. Fancy digs for a fancy lady, he thought. Thick carpet, lots of glass, soft-colored, cushy chairs in the waiting area. Original paintings on the walls, live, thriving plants.

And her secretary, or assistant, or whatever title the pretty little thing at the lobby desk carried, worked with top-grade equipment.

The boss's office was no surprise, either. Ry's quick scan showed him more thick carpet, in slate blue, rosy walls decorated with the splashy modern art he'd never cared for. Antique furniture—probably the real thing.

Her desk was some old European piece, he supposed. They went in for all that gingerbread work and curves. Natalie sat behind it, in one of her tidy suits, a wide, tinted window at her back.

Three other people stood like soldiers ready to snap to attention at her command. He recognized the younger man as the one she'd embraced at the fire site. Tailored suit, shiny leather shoes, ruthlessly knotted tie. Pretty face, blow-dried hair, soft hands.

The second man was older, and looked to be on the edge of a smile. He wore a polka-dot bow tie and a mediocre toupee.

The woman made a fine foil for her boss. Boxy jacket—slightly wrinkled—flat-heeled shoes, messy hair that couldn't decide if it wanted to be red or brown. Closing in on forty, Ry judged, and not much interested in fighting it.

"Inspector," Natalie waited a full ten seconds before rising and holding out a hand.

"Ms. Fletcher." He gave her long, narrow fingers a perfunctory squeeze.

"Inspector Piasecki is investigating the warehouse fire." And in his usual uniform of jeans and a flannel shirt, she noted. Didn't the city issue official attire? "Inspector, these are three of my top-level executives—Donald Hawthorne, Melvin Glasky and Deirdre Marks."

Ry nodded at the introductions, then turned his attention to Natalie again. "I'd have thought a smart woman like you would know better than to put her office on the forty-second floor."

"I beg your pardon?"

"It makes rescue hell—not only for you, but for the department. No way to get a ladder up here. That window's for looks, not for ventilation or escape. You've got forty-two floors to get down, in a stairway that's liable to be filled with smoke."

Natalie sat again, without asking him to join her. "This building is equipped with all necessary safety devices. Sprinklers, smoke detectors, extinguishers."

He only smiled. "So was your warehouse, Ms. Fletcher."

Her headache was coming back, double-time. "Inspector, did you come here to update me on your investigation, or to criticize my work space?"

"I can do both."

"If you'll excuse us." Natalie glanced toward her three associates. Once the door had closed behind them, Natalie gestured to a chair. "Let's clear the air here. You don't like me, I don't like you. But we both have a common goal. Very often I have to work with people I don't care for on a personal level. It doesn't stop me from doing my job." She tilted her head, aimed what he considered a very cool, very regal stare at him. "Does it stop you?"

He crossed his scuffed hightops at the ankles. "Nope."

"Good. Now what do you have to tell me?"

"I've just filed my report. You no longer have a suspicious fire. You've got arson."

Despite the fact that she'd been expecting it, her stomach clutched once. "There's no question?" She shook her head before he could speak. "No, there wouldn't be. I've been told you're very thorough."

"Have you? You ought to try aspirin, before you rub a hole in your head."

Annoyed, Natalie dropped the hand she'd been using to massage her temple. "What's the next step?"

"I've got cause, method, point of origin. I want motive."

"Aren't there people who set fires simply because they enjoy it? Because they're compelled to?"

"Sure." He started to reach for a cigarette, then noticed there wasn't an ashtray in sight. "Maybe you've got a garden-variety spark. Or maybe you've got a hired torch. You were carrying a lot of insurance, Ms. Fletcher."

"That's right. I had a reason for it. I lost over a million and a half in merchandise and equipment alone."

"You were covered for a hell of a lot more."

"If you know anything at all about real estate, Inspector, you're aware that the building was quite valuable. If you're looking for insurance fraud, you're wasting your time."

"I've got time." He rose. "I'm going to need a statement, Ms. Fletcher. Official. Tomorrow, my office, two o'clock."

She rose, as well. "I can give you a statement here and now."

"My office, Ms. Fletcher." He took a card out of his pocket, set it on her desk. "Look at it this way. If you're in the clear, the sooner we get this done, the sooner you collect your insurance."

"Very well." She picked up the card and slipped it into the pocket of her suit. "The sooner the better. Is that all for the moment, Inspector?"

"Yeah." His eyes skimmed down to the cover of the catalog lying on the desk. An ivory-skinned model was curled over a velvet settee, showing off a backless red gown with a froth of tantalizing lace at the bodice.

"Nice." His gaze shot back to Natalie's. "A classy way to sell sex."

"Romance, Inspector. Some people still enjoy it."

"Do you?"

"I don't think that applies."

"I just wondered if you believe in what you're selling, or if you just go for the bucks." Just as he'd wondered if she wore her own products under those neatly tailored suits.

"Then I'll satisfy your curiosity. I always believe in what I'm selling. And I enjoy making money. I'm very good at it." She picked up the catalog and held it out to him. "Why don't you take this along? All our merchandise is unconditionally guaranteed. The toll-free number will be in full operation on Monday."

If she'd expected him to refuse or fumble, she was disappointed. Ry rolled the catalog into a tube and tucked it into his hip pocket. "Thanks."

"Now, if you'll excuse me, I have an outside appointment."

She stepped out from behind the desk. He'd been hoping for that. Whatever he thought about her, he enjoyed her legs. "Need a lift?"

Surprised, she turned away from the small closet at the end of the room. "No. I have a car." It more than surprised her when he came up behind her to help her on with her coat. His hands lingered lightly, briefly, on her shoulders.

"You're stressed out, Ms. Fletcher."

"I'm busy, Inspector." She turned, off balance, and was annoyed when she had to jerk back or bump up against him.

"And jumpy," he added, with a quick, satisfied curve of his lips. He'd wondered if she was as elementally aware of him as he was of her. "A suspicious man might say those were signs of guilt. It so happens I'm a suspicious man. But you know what I think?"

"I'm fascinated by what you think."

Sarcasm apparently had no effect on him. He just continued to smile at her. "I think you're just made up that way. Tense and jumpy. You've got plenty of control, and you know just how to keep the fires banked. But now and again it slips. It's interesting when it does."

It was slipping now. She could feel it sliding

greasily out of her hands. "Do you know what I think, Inspector?"

The dimple that should have been out of place on his strong face winked. "I'm fascinated by what you think, Ms. Fletcher."

"I think you're an arrogant, narrow-minded, irritating man who thinks entirely too much of himself."

"I'd say we're both right."

"And you're in my way."

"You're right about that, too." But he didn't move, wasn't quite ready to. "Damned if you don't have the fanciest face."

She blinked. "I beg your pardon?"

"An observation. You're one classy number." His fingers itched to touch, so he dipped them into his pockets. He'd thrown her off. That was obvious from the way she was staring at him, half horrified, half intrigued. Ry saw no reason not to take advantage of it. "A man's hard-pressed not to do a little fantasizing, once he's had a good look at you. I've had a couple of good looks now."

"I don't think…" Only sheer pride prevented her stepping back. Or forward. "I don't think this is appropriate."

"If we ever get to know each other better, you'll

find out that propriety isn't at the top of my list. Tell me, do you and Hawthorne have a personal thing going?"

His eyes, dark, intense, close, dazzled her for a moment. "Donald? Of course not." Appalled, she caught herself. "That's none of your business."

Her answer pleased him, on professional and personal levels. "Everything about you is my business."

She tossed up her chin, eyes smoldering. "So, this pitiful excuse for a flirtation is just a way to get me to incriminate myself?"

"I didn't think it was that pitiful. Obvious," he admitted, "but not pitiful. On a professional level, it worked."

"I could have lied."

"You have to think before you lie. And you weren't thinking." He liked the idea of being able to frazzle her, and pushed a little farther. "It so happens that, on a strictly personal level, I like the way you look. But don't worry, it won't get in the way of the job."

"I don't like you, Inspector Piasecki."

"You said that already." For his own pleasure, he reached out, tugged her coat closed. "Button up. It's cold out there. My office," he added as he turned for the door. "Tomorrow, two o'clock."

He strolled out, thinking of her.

Natalie Fletcher, he mused, punching the elevator button for the lobby. High-class brains in a first-class package. Maybe she'd torched her own building for a quick profit. She wouldn't be the first or the last.

But his instincts told him no.

She didn't strike him as a woman who looked for shortcuts.

He stepped into the elevator car, which tossed his own image back to him in smoked glass.

Everything about her was top-of-the-line. And her background just didn't equal fraud. Fletcher Industries generated enough profit annually to buy a couple of small Third World countries. This new arm of it was Natalie's baby, and even if it folded in the first year, it wouldn't shake the corporate foundations.

Of course, there was emotional attachment to be considered. Those same instincts told him she had a great deal of emotional attachment to this new endeavor. That was enough for some to try to eke out a quick profit to save a shaky investment.

But it didn't jibe. Not with her.

Someone else in the company, maybe. A competitor, hoping to sabotage her business before it got off the ground. Or a classic pyro, looking for a thrill.

Whatever it was, he'd find it.

And, he thought, he was going to enjoy rattling Natalie Fletcher's cage while he was going about it.

One classy lady, he mused. He imagined she'd look good—damn good—modeling her own merchandise.

The beeper hooked to his belt sounded as he stepped from the elevator. Another fire, he thought, and moved quickly to the nearest phone.

There was always another fire.

Chapter 3

Ry kept her cooling her heels for fifteen minutes. It was a standard ploy, one she'd often used herself to psych out an opponent. She was determined not to fall for it.

There wasn't even enough room in the damn closet he called an office to pace.

He worked in one of the oldest fire stations in the city, two floors above the engines and trucks, in a small glassed-in box that offered an uninspiring view of a cracked parking lot and sagging tenements.

In the adjoining room, Natalie could see a

woman pecking listlessly at a computer keyboard that sat on a desk overflowing with files and forms. The walls throughout were a dingy yellow that might, decades ago, have been white. They were checkerboarded with photos of fire scenes—some of which were grim enough to have had her turning away—bulletins, flyers, and a number of Polish jokes in dubious taste.

Obviously Ry had no problem shrugging off the clichéd humor about his heritage.

Metal shelves were piled with books, binders, pamphlets, and a couple of trophies, each topped with a statuette of a basketball player. And, she noted with a sniff, dust. His desk, slightly larger than a card table and badly scarred, was propped up under one shortened leg by a tattered paperback copy of *The Red Pony*.

The man didn't even have respect for Steinbeck.

When her curiosity got the better of her, Natalie rose from the folding chair, with its torn plastic seat, and poked around his desk.

No photographs, she noted. No personal mementos. Bent paper clips, broken pencils, a claw hammer, a ridiculous mess of disorganized paperwork. She pushed at some of that, then jumped back in horror when she revealed the decapitated head of a doll.

She might have laughed at herself, if it wasn't so hideous. The remnant of a child's toy, the frizzy blond hair nearly burned away, the once rosy face melted into mush on one side. One bright blue eye remained staring.

"Souvenirs," Ry said from the doorway. He'd been watching her for a couple of minutes. "From a class A fire up in the east sixties. The kid made it." He glanced down at the head on his desk. "She was in a little better shape than her doll."

Her shudder was quick and uncontrollable. "That's horrible."

"Yeah, it was. The kid's father started it with a can of kerosene in the living room. The wife wanted a divorce. When he was finished, she didn't need one."

He was so cold about it, she thought. Maybe he had to be. "You have a miserable job, Inspector."

"That's why I love it." He glanced around as the outer door opened. "Have a seat. I'll be right with you." Ry pulled the office door closed before he turned to the uniformed firefighter who'd come in behind him.

Through the glass, Natalie could hear the mutter of voices. She didn't need to hear Ry raise his voice—as he soon did—to know that the young fireman was receiving a first-class dressing-down.

"Who told you to ventilate that wall, probie?"

"Sir, I thought—"

"Probies don't think. You're not smart enough to think. If you were, you'd know what fresh air does for a fire. You'd know what happens when you let it in and there's a damn puddle of fuel oil sloshing under your boots."

"Yes, sir. I know, sir. I didn't see it. The smoke—"

"You'd better learn to see through smoke. You'd better learn to see through everything. And when the fire goes into the frigging wall, you don't take it on yourself to give it a way out while you're standing in accelerant. You're lucky to be alive, probie, and so's the team who were unlucky enough to be with you."

"Yes, sir. I know, sir."

"You don't know diddly. That's the first thing you remember the next time you go in to eat smoke. Now get out of here."

Natalie crossed her legs when Ry came into the room. "You're a real diplomat. That kid couldn't have been more than twenty."

"Be nice if he lived to a ripe old age, wouldn't it?" With a flick of his wrist, Ry tugged down the blinds, closing them in.

"Your technique makes me regret I didn't bring a lawyer with me."

"Relax." He moved to his desk, pushed some files out of his way. "I don't have the authority to arrest, just to investigate."

"Well, I'll sleep easy now." Deliberately she took a long look at her watch. "How long do you think this is going to take? I've already wasted twenty minutes."

"I got held up." He sat, opened the bag he'd brought in with him. "Have you had lunch?"

"No." Her eyes narrowed as he took out a wrapped package that smelled tantalizingly of deli. "Are you telling me that you've kept me waiting in here while you picked up a sandwich?"

"It was on my way." He offered her half of a corned beef on rye. "I've got a couple of coffees, too."

"I'll take the coffee. Keep the sandwich."

"Suit yourself." He handed her a small insulated cup. "Mind if we record this?"

"I'd prefer it."

Eating with one hand, he opened a desk drawer,

took out a tape recorder. "You must have a closet full of those suits." This one was the color of crushed raspberries, and fastened at the left hip with gold buttons. "Do you ever wear anything else?"

"I beg your pardon?"

"Small talk, Ms. Fletcher."

"I'm not here for small talk," she snapped back. "And stop calling me *Ms.* Fletcher in that irritating way."

"No problem, Natalie. Just call me Ry." He switched on the recorder and began by reciting the time, date and location of the interview. Despite the tape, he took out a notebook and pencil. "This interview is being conducted by Inspector Ryan Piasecki with Natalie Fletcher, re the fire at the Fletcher Industries warehouse, 21 South Harbor Avenue, on February 12 of this year."

He took a sip of his coffee. "Ms. Fletcher, you are the owner of the aforesaid building, and its contents."

"The building and its contents are—were—the property of Fletcher Industries, of which I am an executive officer."

"How long has the building belonged to your company?"

"For eight years. It was previously used to warehouse inventory for Fletcher Shipping."

The heater beside him began to whine and gurgle. Ry kicked it carelessly. It went back to a subdued hum.

"And now?"

"Fletcher Shipping moved to a new location." She relaxed a little. It was going to be routine now. Business. "The warehouse was converted nearly two years ago to accommodate a new company. We used the building for manufacturing and warehousing merchandise for Lady's Choice. We make ladies' lingerie."

"And what were the hours of operation?"

"Normally eight to six, Monday through Friday. In the last six months, we expanded that to include Saturdays from eight to noon."

He continued to eat, asking standard questions about business practices, security, vandalism. Her answers were quick, cool and concise.

"You have a number of suppliers."

"Yes. We use American companies only. That's a firm policy."

"Ups the overhead."

"In the short term. I believe, in the long term, the company will generate profits to merit it."

"You've put a lot of personal time into this company. Incurred a lot of expenses, invested your own money."

"That's right."

"What happens if the business doesn't live up to your expectations?"

"It will."

He leaned back now, enjoying what was left of his cooling coffee. "If it doesn't."

"Then I would lose my time, and my money."

"When was the last time you were in the building, before the fire?"

The sudden change of topic surprised but didn't throw her. "I went by for a routine check three days before the fire. That would have been the ninth of February."

He noted it down. "Did you notice any inventory missing?"

"No."

"Damaged equipment?"

"No."

"Any holes in security?"

"No. I would have dealt with any of those things immediately." Did he think she was an idiot? "Work was progressing on schedule, and the inventory I looked over was fine."

His eyes cut back to hers, lingered. "You didn't look over everything?"

"I did a spot check, Inspector." The stare was designed to make her uncomfortable, she knew. She refused to allow it. "It isn't a productive use of time for me or my staff to examine every negligee or garter belt."

"The building was inspected in November. You were up to code on all fire regulations."

"That's right."

"Can you explain how it was that, on the night of the fire, the sprinkler and smoke alarm systems were inoperative?"

"Inoperative?" Her heart picked up a beat. "I'm not sure what you mean."

"They were tampered with, Ms. Fletcher. So was your security system."

She kept her eyes level with his. "No, I can't explain it. Can you?"

He took out a cigarette, flicked a wooden match into flame with his thumbnail. "Do you have any enemies?"

Her face went blank. "Enemies?"

"Anyone who'd like to see you fail, personally or professionally?"

"I— No, I can't think of anyone, personally."

The idea left her shaken. She pulled a hand through her hair, from the crown to the tips that swung at chin level. "Naturally, I have competitors...."

"Anyone who's given you trouble?"

"No."

"Disgruntled employees? Fire anyone lately?"

"No. I can't speak for every level of the organization. I have managers who have autonomy in their own departments, but nothing's come back to me."

He continued to smoke as he asked questions, took notes. He wound the interview down, closing it by logging the time.

"I spoke to your insurance adjuster this morning," he told her. "And your security guard. I have interviews set up with the foremen at the warehouse." When she didn't respond, he crushed out his cigarette. "Want some water?"

"No." She let out a breath. "Thank you. Do you think I'm responsible?"

"What I know goes into the report, not what I think."

"I want to know." She stood then. "I'm asking you to tell me what you think."

She didn't belong here. That was the first

thought that crossed his mind. Not here, in the cramped little room that smelled of whatever the men were cooking downstairs. Boardrooms and bedrooms. He was certain she'd be equally adept in both venues.

"I don't know, Natalie, maybe it's your pretty face affecting my judgment, but no—I don't think you're responsible. Feel better?"

"Not much. I suppose my only choice now is to depend on you to find out the who and why." She let out a little sigh. "As much as it galls me, I have a feeling you're just the man for the job."

"A compliment, and so early in our relationship."

"With any luck, it'll be the first and the last." She shifted, reached down for her briefcase. He moved quickly and quietly. Before she could lift it, his hand closed over hers on the strap.

"Take a break."

She flexed her hand under his once, felt the hard, callused palm, then went still. "Excuse me?"

"You're revved, Natalie, but you're running on empty. You need to relax."

It was unlikely she would, or could, with him holding on to her. "What I need to do is get back to work. So, if that's all, Inspector…"

"I thought we were on a first-name basis now. Come on, I want to show you something."

"I don't have time," she began as he pulled her out of the room. "I have an appointment."

"You always seem to. Aren't you ever late?"

"No."

"Every man's fantasy woman. Beautiful, smart, and prompt." He led her down a staircase. "How tall are you without the stilts?"

She lifted a brow at his description of her elegant Italian pumps. "Tall enough."

He stopped, one step below her, and turned. They were lined up, eye to eye, mouth to mouth. "Yeah, I'd say you are, just tall enough."

He tugged her, as he might have a disinterested mule, until they reached the ground floor.

There were scents wafting out from the kitchen. Chili was on the menu for tonight. A couple of men were checking equipment on one of the engines. Another was rolling a hose on the chilly concrete floor.

Ry was greeted with salutes and quick grins, Natalie with pursed lips and groans.

"They can't help it," Ry told her. "We don't get legs like yours walking through here every day. I'll give you a boost."

"What?"

"I'll give you a boost," he repeated as he opened the door on an engine. "Not that the guys wouldn't appreciate the way that skirt would ride up if you climbed in on your own. But—" Before she could protest, Ry had gripped her by the waist and lifted her.

She had a moment to think the strength in his arms was uncannily effortless before he joined her.

"Move over," he ordered. "Unless you'd rather sit on my lap."

She scooted across the seat. "Why am I sitting in a fire engine?"

"Everybody wants to at least once." Very much at home, he stretched his arm over the seat. "So, what do you think?"

She scanned the gauges and dials, the oversize gearshift, the photo of Miss January taped to the dash. "It's interesting."

"That's it?"

She caught her bottom lip between her teeth. She wondered which control operated the siren, which the lights. "Okay, it's fun." She leaned forward for a better view through the windshield. "We're really up here, aren't we? Is this the—"

He caught her hand just before she could yank the cord over her head. "Horn," he finished. "The men are used to it, but believe me, with the acoustics in here and the outside doors shut, you'd be sorry if you sounded it."

"Too bad." She skimmed back her hair as she turned her face toward him. "Are you showing me your toy to relax me, or just to show off?"

"Both. How'm I doing?"

"Maybe you're not quite the jerk you appear to be."

"You keep being so nice to me, I'm going to fall in love."

She laughed and realized she was almost relaxed. "I think we're both safe on that count. What made you decide to sit in a fire engine for ten years?"

"You've been checking up on me." Idly he lifted his fingers, just enough to reach the tips of her hair. Soft, he thought, like sunny silk.

"That's right." She shot him a look. "So?"

"So, I guess we're even. I'm a third-generation smoke eater. It's in the blood."

"Mmm…" That she understood. "But you gave it up."

"No, I shifted gears. That's different."

She supposed it was, but it wasn't a real answer. "Why do you keep that souvenir on your desk?" She watched his eyes closely as she asked. "The doll's head."

"It's from my last fire. The last one I fought." He could still remember it—the heat, the smoke, the screaming. "I carried the kid out. The bedroom door was locked. My guess is he'd herded his wife and kid in—you know, you can't live with me, you won't live without me. He had a gun. It wasn't loaded, but she wouldn't have known that."

"That's horrible." She wondered if she would have risked the gun, and thought she would have. Better a bullet, fast and final, than the terrors of smoke and flame. "His own family."

"Some guys don't take kindly to divorce." He shrugged. His own had been painless enough, almost anticlimactic. "The way it came out, he made them sit there while the fire got bigger, and the smoke snuck under the door. It was a frame house, old. Went up like a matchstick. The woman had tried to protect the kid, had curled over her in a corner. I couldn't get them both at once, so I took the kid."

His eyes changed now, darkened, focused on something only he could see. "The woman was gone, anyway. I knew she was gone, but there's always a chance. I was headed down the steps with the kid when the floor gave way."

"You saved the child," Natalie said gently.

"The mother saved the child." He could never forget that, could never forget that selfless and hopeless devotion. "The son of a bitch who torched the house jumped out the second-story window. Oh, he was burned, smoke inhalation, broken leg. But he lived through it."

He cared, she realized. She hadn't seen that before. Or hadn't wanted to. It changed him. Changed her perception of him. "And you decided to go after the men who start them, instead of the fires themselves."

"More or less." He snapped his head up, like a wolf scenting prey, when the alarm shrilled. The station sprang to life with running feet, shouted orders. Ry pitched his voice over the din. "Let's get out of the way."

He pushed open the door, caught Natalie in one arm and swung out.

"Chemical plant," someone said as they hurried by, pulling on protective gear.

In seconds, it seemed, the engines were manned and screaming out the arched double doors.

"It's so fast," Natalie said, ears still ringing, pulse still jumping. "They move so fast."

"Yeah."

"It's exciting." She pressed a hand to her speeding heart. "I didn't realize. Do you miss it?" She looked up at him then, and her hand went limp.

He was still holding her against him, and his eyes were dark and focused on hers. "Now and again."

"Well, it's— I should go."

"Yeah. You should go." But he shifted her until she was wrapped in both his arms. Maybe it was a knee-jerk reaction to the sirens, maybe it was the exotic and irresistible scent of her, but his blood was pumping.

And he wanted to see, just once, if she tasted as good as she looked.

"This is insane," she managed to say. She knew what he intended to do. What she wanted him to do. "This has got to be wrong."

His lips curved, just a little. "What's your point?" Then his mouth closed over hers.

She didn't push back. For nearly one heartbeat, she didn't respond. In that instant she thought she'd been paralyzed, struck deaf, dumb and blind. Then, in a tidal wave, every sense flooded back, every nerve snapped, every pulse jolted.

His mouth was hard, as his hands were, as his body was. She felt terrifyingly, gloriously, feminine pressed against him. A need she hadn't been aware of exploded into bloom. Her briefcase hit the floor with a thud as she wrapped herself around him.

He was no longer thinking "just once." A man would starve to death after only one taste. A man would certainly beg for more. She was soft and strong and sinfully sweet, with a flavor that both tempted and tormented.

Heat radiated between them as the wind whipped in through the open doors at their back. The clatter of street noises, horns and tires, sounded around them, along with her dazed, throaty moan.

He pulled back once to look at her face, saw himself in the cloudy green of her eyes, and then his mouth crushed hers again.

No, this wasn't going to happen just once.

She couldn't breathe. No longer wanted to. His lips were moving against hers, forming words she could neither hear nor understand. For the first time in her memory, she could do nothing but feel. And the feelings came so fast, so sharp and strong, they left her in tatters.

He pulled back again, staggered by what had ripped through him in so short a time. He was winded, weak, and the sensation infuriated as much as it baffled him. She only stood there, staring at him with a mixture of shock and hunger in her eyes.

"Sorry," he muttered, and hooked his thumbs in his pockets.

"Sorry?" she repeated. She sucked in a deep breath, wondered if her head would ever stop spinning. *"Sorry?"*

"That's right." He couldn't decide whether to curse her or himself. Damn it, his knees were weak. "That was out of line."

"Out of line."

She brushed her hair back from her face, furious to find her skin heated. He'd torn aside every defense, every line of control, and now he dared to apologize? Her chin snapped up, her shoulders straightened.

"You've certainly got a way with words. Tell me, Inspector, do you paw all your suspects?"

His eyes narrowed, kindled. "It was mutual pawing, and no, you're the first."

"Lucky me." Amazed, appalled, that she was very near tears, Natalie snatched up her briefcase. "I believe this concludes our meeting."

"Hold it." Ryan played fair and cursed them both when she continued striding toward the doors. "I said, hold it." He headed after her, and with one hand on her arm he spun her around.

Her breath hissed out between clenched teeth. "I refuse to give in to the typical cliché of slapping you, but it's costing me."

"I apologized."

"Stuff it."

Be reasonable, he cautioned himself. It was either that or kiss her again. "Look, Ms. Fletcher, you didn't exactly fight me off."

"A mistake, I assure you, that will not be repeated." She made it to the sidewalk this time before he caught her.

"I don't want you," he said definitely.

Insulted, provoked beyond her control, she jabbed a finger into his chest. "Oh, really? Then perhaps you'd care to explain that ham-handed maneuver in there?"

"There was nothing ham-handed about it. I hardly touched you, and you went off like a rocket. It's not my fault if you were ripe."

Her eyes went huge, ballistic. "Ripe? *Ripe?* Why you—you overbearing, arrogant self-absorbed idiot!"

"Tell him, honey" was the advice of a toothy bag lady who shoved past with her teetering cart. "Don't let him get away with it."

"That was a bad choice of words," Ry responded, goaded into adding more fuel to the fire. "I should have said *repressed.*"

"I am going to hit you."

"And," he continued, ignoring her, "I should have said I don't like wanting you."

Natalie concentrated for one moment on simply breathing. She would not, absolutely would not, lower herself to having a public brawl on the sidewalk. "That, Inspector Piasecki, may be the first and last time we ever have the same sentiment about anything. I don't like it, either."

"Don't like me wanting you, or don't like you wanting me?"

"Either."

He nodded, and they eyed each other like boxers between rounds. "So, we'll talk it out tonight."

"We will not."

He would, he promised himself, be patient if it killed him. Or her. "Natalie, just how complicated do you want to make this?"

"I don't want to make it complicated, *Ry.* I want to make it impossible."

"Why?"

She speared him with a look, skimming her gaze from the toes of his shoes to the top of his head. "I should think that would be obvious, even to you."

He rocked back on his heels. "I don't know what it is about that snotty attitude of yours—it just does something for me. You want to play this traditional, with me asking you out to dinner, that routine?"

She closed her eyes and prayed for patience. "I don't seem to be getting through." She opened them again. "No, I don't want you asking me out to dinner, or any routine. What happened inside there was—"

"Wild. Incredible."

"An aberration," she said between her teeth.

"It wouldn't be a hardship to prove you wrong. But if we started that again out here, we'd probably be arrested before we were finished." Ryan was enjoying himself now, immersed in the simple challenge of her. And he intended to win. "But I see what it is. I've spooked you. Now you're afraid to be alone with me, afraid you'll lose control."

Heat stung her cheeks. "That's very lame."

He shrugged. "Works for me."

She studied him. He wanted to prove something? He was about to be disappointed. "All right. Eight o'clock. Chez Robert, on Third. I'll meet you there."

"Fine."

"Fine." She turned away. "Oh, Piasecki," she called over her shoulder. "They frown on eating with your fingers."

"I'll keep it in mind."

Natalie was sure she had lost her mind. She dashed into her apartment at 7:15. Facts, figures, projections, graphs, were all running through her head. And her phone was ringing.

She caught the cordless on the fly and dashed into the bedroom to change. "Yes? What?"

"Is that how Mom taught you to answer the phone?"

"Boyd." Some of the tension of the day drained away at the sound of her brother's voice. "I'm sorry. I've just come in from the last of several mind-numbing meetings."

"Don't look for sympathy here. You're the one who opted to carry on the family tradition."

"Right you are." She stepped out of her shoes.

"So how's the fight against crime and corruption in Denver, Captain Fletcher?"

"We're holding our own. Cilla and the kids send love, kisses and so forth."

"And send mine back at them. Aren't they going to talk to me?"

"I'm at the station. I'm a little concerned about crime out there in Urbana."

She searched through her closet, the phone caught in the curve of her shoulder. "How did you find out the fire was arson already? I barely found out myself."

"We have ways. Actually, I just got off the phone with the investigator in charge."

"Piasecki?" Natalie tossed a black dinner dress on her bed. "You talked to him?"

"Ten minutes ago. It sounds like you're in good hands, Nat."

"Not if I can help it," she muttered.

"What?"

"He appears to know his job," she said calmly. "Though his methods lack a certain style."

"Arson's a dirty business. And a dangerous one. I'm worried about you, pal."

"Don't be. You're the cop, remember." She struggled out of her jacket, promising herself she'd hang it up before she left. "I'm the CEO in the ivory tower."

"I've never known you to stay there. I want you to keep me up-to-date on the investigation."

"I can do that." She wiggled out of her skirt, and guiltily left it pooled on the floor. "And tell Mom and Dad, if you talk to them before I do, that things are under control. I won't bore you with all the business data—"

"I appreciate that."

She grinned. Boyd had no patience with ledgers or bar graphs. "But I'm about to put another very colorful feather in the Fletcher Industries cap."

"With underwear."

"Lingerie, darling." A little breathless, she fastened on a strapless black bra. "You can buy underwear at a drugstore."

"Right. Well, I can tell you on a personal level, Cilla and I have both thoroughly enjoyed the samples you sent out. I particularly liked the little red thing with the tiny hearts."

"I thought you would." She stepped into the dress, tugged it up to her hips. "With Valentine's Day coming up, you should think about ordering her the matching peignoir."

"Put it on my tab. Take care of yourself, Nat."

"I intend to. With any luck, I'll be seeing you next month. I'm going to scout out locations in Denver."

"Your room's ready for you anytime. And so are we. I love you."

"I love you, too. Bye."

She hung up by dropping the phone on the bed, freeing herself to zip the dress into place. Not exactly a sedate number, she mused, turning toward the mirror. Not with the way it draped off the shoulders and veed down over the curve of the breasts.

Repressed? She shook back her hair. This ought to show him.

The phone rang again, making her swear in disgust. She ignored the first ring and picked up her brush. By the third, she'd given up and pounced on the phone.

"Hello?"

Just breathing, quick, and a faint chuckle.

"Hello? Is someone there?"

"Midnight."

"What?" Distracted, she carried the phone to the dresser to select the right jewelry. "I'm sorry, I didn't catch that."

"Midnight. Witching hour. Wait and see."

When the phone clicked, she disconnected, set it down with a shake of her head. Cranks.

"Use the answering machine, Natalie," she ordered herself. "That's what it's there for."

A glance at her watch had her swearing again. She forgot the call as she went into grooming overdrive. She absolutely refused to be late.

Chapter 4

Natalie arrived at Chez Robert precisely at eight. The four-star French restaurant, with its floral walls and candlelit corners, had been a favorite of hers since she relocated to Urbana. Just stepping inside put her at ease. She had no more than checked her coat when she was greeted enthusiastically by the maître d'.

He kissed her hand with a flourish and beamed. "Ah, Mademoiselle Fletcher...a pleasure, as always. I didn't know you were dining with us this evening."

"I'm meeting a companion, André. A Mr. Piasecki."

"Pi…" Brows knit, André scanned his reservation book while he mentally sounded out the name. "Ah, yes, two for eight o'clock. Pizekee."

"Close enough," Natalie murmured.

"Your companion has not yet arrived, *mademoiselle*. Let me escort you to your table." With a few quick and ruthless adjustments, André shifted Ryan's reservation to suit his favorite customer, moving the seating from a small central table in the main traffic pattern to Natalie's favorite quiet corner booth.

"Thank you, André." Already at home, Natalie settled into the booth with a little sigh. Beneath the table, her feet slipped out of her shoes.

"My pleasure, as always. Would you care for a drink while you wait?"

"A glass of champagne, thank you. My usual."

"Of course. Right away. And, *mademoiselle,* if I may be so presumptuous, the lobster Robert, tonight it is…" He kissed his fingers.

"I'll keep that in mind."

While she waited, Natalie took out her date book and began to make notations on her schedule for the next day. She had nearly finished her champagne when Ry walked up to the table.

She didn't bother to glance up. "It's a good thing I'm not a fire."

"I'm never late for a fire." He took his seat, and they spent a moment measuring each other.

So, he owned a suit, Natalie thought. And he looked good in it. Dark jacket, crisp white shirt, subtle gray tie. Even though his hair wasn't quite tamed, it was definitely a more classic look than she'd expected from him.

"I use it for funerals," Ry said, reading her perfectly.

She only lifted a brow. "Well, that certainly sets the tone for the evening, doesn't it?"

"You picked the spot," he reminded her. He glanced around the restaurant. Quiet class, he mused. Just a tad ornate and stuffy—exactly what he'd expected. "So, how's the food here?"

"It's excellent."

"Mademoiselle Fletcher." Robert himself, small, plump, and tuxedoed, stopped by the table to kiss Natalie's hand. *"Bienvenue…"* he began.

Ry sat back, took out a cigarette and watched as they rattled away in French. She spoke it like a native. That, too, he'd expected.

"Du champagne pour mademoiselle," Robert told the waiter. *"Et pour vous, monsieur?"*

"Beer," Ry said. "American, if you've got it."

"Bien sûr." Robert strutted back to the kitchen to harass his chef.

"Well, Legs, that should have made your point," Ry commented.

"Excuse me?"

"Just how out of place will he be in a fancy French restaurant where the owner kisses your knuckles and asks after your family?"

"I don't know what you're—" Natalie frowned as she picked up her glass. "How do you know he asked after my family?"

"I have a French-Canadian grandmother. I probably speak the lingo nearly as well as you do, even if the accent isn't as classy." He blew out a stream of smoke and smiled at her through it. "I didn't peg you as a snob, Natalie."

"I certainly am not a snob." Insulted, she set her glass down again, her shoulders stiffening. But when he only continued to smile, a little frisson of guilt worked its way through her conscience. "Maybe I wanted to make you a little uncomfortable." She sighed, gave up. "A lot uncomfortable. You annoyed me."

"I did better than that." Angling his head, he gave her a long, slow study. She looked like something a man might beg for. Creamy skin flowing out of a black dress, just a few sparkles here and there, sleek golden hair curving around her face. Big, sulky green eyes, red mouth.

Oh, yes, he decided. A man would surely beg.

Her nerves began to jangle as he continued to stare. "Is there a problem?"

"No, no problem. Did you wear that dress to make me uncomfortable?"

"Yes."

He picked up his menu. "It's working. How's the steak here?"

Relax, she ordered herself. Obviously he was trying to make her crazy. "You won't get better in the city. Though I generally prefer the seafood."

She pouted a bit as she studied her menu. The evening was not going as she'd planned. Not only had he seen through her, but he'd already turned the tables so that she looked and felt foolish. Try again, she told herself, and make the best of a bad deal.

After they'd given their orders, Natalie took a deep breath. "I suppose, since we're here, we might as well have a truce."

"Were we fighting?"

"Let's just try for a pleasant evening." She picked up her champagne flute again, sipped. She was, after all, an expert in negotiations and diplomacy. "Let's start with the obvious. Your name. Irish first, Eastern European last."

"Irish mother, Polish father."

"And a French-Canadian grandmother."

"On my mother's side. My other grandmother's a Scot."

"Which makes you—"

"An all-American boy. You've got high-tea hands." He picked up her hand, startling her by running his fingers down hers. "They go with your name. Upper-crust. Classy."

"Well." After she'd tugged her hand free, she cleared her throat, giving undue attention to buttering a roll. "You said you were third-generation in the department."

"Do I make you nervous when I touch you?"

"Yes. Let's try to keep this simple."

"Why?"

Since she had no ready answer for that, she let out a little huff of relief when their appetizers were served. "You must have always wanted to be a firefighter."

All right, he decided, they could cruise along at her speed for now. "Sure I did. I practically grew up at engine company 19, where my pop worked."

"I imagine there was some family pressure."

"No. How about you?"

"Me?"

"The Fletcher tradition. Big business, corporate towers." He lifted a brow. "Family pressure?"

"Plenty of it," she said, and smiled. "Ruthless, unbending, determined. And all from my corner." Her eyes glinted with amusement. "It had always been assumed that my brother Boyd would take over the reins. Both he and I had different ideas about that. So he strapped on a badge and a gun, and I harassed my parents into accepting me as heir apparent."

"They objected?"

"No, not really. It didn't take them long to realize I was serious. And capable." She took a last bite of her coquilles Saint-Jacques and offered Ry the rest. "I love business. The wheeling, the dealing, the paperwork, the meetings. And this new company. It's all mine."

"Your catalog's a big hit down at the station."

The amusement settled in, and felt comfortable. "Oh, really?"

"A lot of the men have wives, or ladies. I'm just helping you pick up a few orders."

"That's generous of you." She studied him over the rim of her glass. "What about you? Are you going to make any orders?"

"I don't have a wife, or a lady." Those smoky eyes flicked over her face again. "At the moment."

"But you did have. A wife."

"Briefly."

"Sorry. I'm prying."

"No problem." He shrugged and finished off his beer. "It's old news. Nearly ten years old. I guess you could say she fell for the uniform, then decided she didn't like the hours I had to be in it."

"Children?"

"No." He regretted that, sometimes wondered if he always would. "We were only together a couple of years. She hooked up with a plumber and moved to the suburbs." He reached out, skimmed a fingertip down the side of her neck, along the curve of her shoulder. "I'm beginning to think I like your shoulders as much as your legs." His eyes locked on hers. "Maybe it's the whole package."

"That's a fascinating compliment." She didn't give in to the urge to shift away, but she did switch from champagne to water. Suddenly her mouth was dry as dust. "But don't you think the current circumstances require a certain professional detachment?"

"No. If I thought you had anything to do with setting that fire, maybe." He liked the way her eyes lit and narrowed when he pushed the right button. "But, as it stands, I can do my job just fine, and still wonder what it would be like to make love with you."

Her pulse jolted, scrambled. She used the time while their entrées were served to steady it. "I'd prefer if you'd concentrate on the first. In fact, if you could bring me up-to-date—"

"Seems a waste to talk shop in a joint like this." But he shrugged his shoulders. "The bottom line is arson, an incendiary fire. The motive could be revenge, money, straight vandalism or malicious destruction. Or kicks."

"A pyromaniac." She preferred that one, only because it was less personal. "How do you handle that?"

"First, you don't go in biased. A lot of times people, and the media, start shouting 'pyro' whenever there's a series of fires. Even if they seem related, it's not always the case."

"But it often is."

"And it's often simple. Somebody burns a dozen cars because he's ticked he bought a lemon."

"So don't jump to conclusions."

"Exactly."

"But if it *is* someone who's disturbed?"

"Head doctors are always working on the whys. Are you going to let me taste that?"

"Hmmm? Oh, all right." She nudged her plate closer to his so that he could sample her lobster. "Do you work with psychiatrists?"

"Mostly the shrinks don't come into it until you've got the firebug in custody. That's good stuff," he added, nodding toward her plate. "Anyway, that could be after any number of fires, months of investigation. Maybe they blame his mother. She paid too much attention to him. Or his father, because he didn't pay enough. You know how it goes."

Amused, interested, she cut off a piece of lobster and slipped it onto his plate. "You don't think much of psychiatry?"

"I didn't say that. I just don't go in for blaming somebody else when you did the crime."

"Now you sound like my brother."

"He's probably a good cop. Want some of this steak?"

"No, thanks." Like a bulldog, she kept her teeth in the topic. "Wouldn't you, as an investigator, have to know something about the psychology of the fire starter?"

Ry chewed his steak, signaled for another beer. "You really want to get into this?"

"It's interesting. Particularly now."

"Okay. Short lesson. You can divide pathological fire starters into four groups. The mentally ill, the psychotic, the neurotic, and the sociopath. You're going to have some overlap most of the time, but that sorts them. The neurotic, or psycho-neurotic, is the pyromaniac."

"Aren't they all?"

"No. The true pyro's a lot rarer than most people think. It's an uncontrollable compulsion. He *has* to set the fire. When the urge hits him, he goes with it, wherever, whenever. He's not really thinking about covering up or getting away, so he's usually easy to catch."

"I thought *pyro* was more of a general term." She started to tuck her hair behind her ear. Ry beat her to it, letting his fingers linger for a moment.

"I like to see your face when I talk to you." He

kept his hand on hers, bringing them both back to the table. "I like to touch you when I talk to you."

Silence hung for a full ten seconds.

"You're not talking," Natalie pointed out.

"Sometimes I just like to look. Come here a minute."

She recognized the light in his eyes, recognized her own helpless response to it. And to him. Deliberately she eased away. "I don't think so. You're a dangerous man, Inspector."

"Thanks. Why don't you come home with me, Natalie?"

She let out a long, quiet breath. "You're also a very blunt one."

"A woman like you could get poetry and fancy moves any time she wanted." Ry neither had them nor believed in them. "You might want to try something more basic."

"This is certainly basic," she agreed. "I think we could use some coffee."

He signaled the waiter. "You didn't answer my question."

"No, I didn't. And no." She waited until the table was cleared, the coffee order given. "Despite a certain elemental attraction, I think it would be unwise to pursue this any further. We're both committed to our careers, diametrically opposed in personality and lifestyle. Even though our relationship has been brief and abrasive, I think it's clear we have nothing in common. We are, as we might say in my business, a bad risk."

He said nothing for a minute, only studied her, as if considering. "That makes sense."

Her stomach muscles relaxed. She even smiled at him as she picked up her coffee. "Good, then we're agreed—"

"I didn't say I agreed," he pointed out. "I said it made sense." He lit a cigarette, his eyes on hers over the flame. "I've been thinking about you, Natalie. And I've got to tell you, I don't much like the way you make me feel. It's distracting, annoying and inconvenient."

Her chin angled. "I'm so glad we cleared this up," she said coolly.

"God knows it gets me right in the gut when you talk to me like that. Duchess to serf." He shook his head, drew in smoke. "I must be perverse. Anyway, I don't like it. I'm not altogether sure I like you." His eyes narrowed, the light in them stopping the pithy comment before it could slip through her lips. "But I've never wanted anyone so damn much in my whole life. That's a problem."

"*Your* problem," she managed.

"Our problem. I've got a rep for being tenacious."

She set her cup down, carefully, before it could slip from her limp fingers. "I'd think a simple no would do, Ry."

"So would I." He shrugged. "Go figure. I haven't been able to clear you out of my head since I saw you standing there freezing at the fire scene. I made a mistake when I kissed you this afternoon. I figured once I had, that would be it. Case closed."

He moved quickly, and so smoothly she barely had time to blink before his mouth was hot and hard on hers. Dazed, she lifted a hand to his shoulder, but her fingers only dug in, held on, as she was buffeted with fresh excitement.

"I was wrong." He drew back. "Case isn't closed, and that's *our* problem."

"Yeah." She let out a shaky breath. No amount of common sense could outweigh her instant and primitive response to him. He touched, she wanted. It was as simple and as terrifying as that. But common sense was her only defense. "This isn't going to work. It's ridiculous to think that it could. I'm not prepared to jump into an affair simply because of some basic animal lust."

"See? We do have something in common." Despite the fact that the kiss had stirred him to aching, he smiled at her. "The lust part."

Laughing, she dragged her hair back from her face. "Oh, I need to get away from you for a while and consider the options."

"This isn't a business deal, Ms. Fletcher."

She looked at him again and wished she could have some distance, just a little distance, so that she could think clearly. "I never make a decision without considering the bottom line."

"Profit and loss?"

Wary, she inclined her head. "In a manner of speaking. You could call it risk and reward. Intimate relationships haven't been my strong suit. That's been my choice. If I'm going to have one with you, however brief, that will be my choice, as well."

"That's fair. Do you want me to work up a prospectus?"

"Don't be snide, Ry." Then, because it soothed some of the tension to realize she'd annoyed him, she smiled. "But I'd certainly give it my full attention." Playing it up, she cupped her chin on her hands, leaning closer, skimming her gaze over his face. "You are very attractive, in a rough-edged, not-quite-tamed sort of way."

He shifted, drew hard on his cigarette. "Thanks a lot."

"No, really." So, she thought, he could be embarrassed. "The faint cleft in the chin, the sharp cheekbones, the lean face, the dark, sexy eyes." Her lips curved as he narrowed those eyes. "And all that hair, just a little unruly. The tough body, the tough attitude."

Impatient, he crushed out his cigarette. "What are you pulling here, Natalie?"

"Just giving you back a little of your own. Yes, you're a very attractive package. Wasn't that your word? Dangerous, dynamic. Like Nemesis."

Now he winced. "Give me a break."

Her chuckle was warm and deep. "No, really. There's a lot of similarity between you and Urbana's mysterious upholder of justice. You both appear to have your own agenda, and your own rough-edged style. He fights crime, appearing and disappearing like smoke. An interesting connection between the two of you.

"I might even wonder if you could be him—except that he's a very romantic figure. And there, Inspector, you part company."

She tossed back her hair and laughed. "I believe

you're speechless. Who would have thought it would be that easy to score a point off you?"

She might have scored one, but the game wasn't over. He caught her chin in his hand, held it steady and close, even as her eyes continued to dance. "I guess I could handle it if you wanted to treat me like an object. Just promise to respect me in the morning."

"Nope."

"You're a hard woman, Ms. Fletcher. Okay, scratch respect. How about awe?"

"I'll consider it. If and when it becomes applicable. Now, why don't we get the check? It's late."

When the check was served, as it always was in such establishments, with a faint air of apology, Natalie reached for it automatically. Ry pushed her hand aside and picked it up himself.

"Ry, I didn't mean for you to pay the tab." Flustered, she watched him pull out a credit card. She knew exactly what a meal cost at Chez Robert, and had a good idea what salary a city employee pulled down. "Really. It was my idea to come here."

"Shut up, Natalie." He figured the tip, signed the stub.

"Now I feel guilty. Damn it, we both know I

picked this place to rub your nose in it. At least let me split it."

He pocketed his wallet. "No." He slid out of the booth, offered his hand. "Don't worry," he said dryly. "I can still make the rent this month. Probably."

"You're just being stubborn," she muttered.

"Where's the ticket for your coat?"

Male ego, she thought on a disgusted sigh as she took the ticket from her purse. She exchanged good-nights with André and Robert before Ry helped her into her coat.

"Do you need a lift?" Ry asked her.

"No, I have my car."

"Good. I don't have mine. You can give me a ride home."

She shot a suspicious look over her shoulder as they stepped outside. "If this is some sort of maneuver, I'll tell you right now, I'm not falling for it."

"Fine. I can take a cab." He scanned the street. "If I can find one. It's a cold night," he added. "Feels like snow on the way."

Her breath streamed out. "My car's in the lot around the corner. Where am I taking you?"

"Twenty-second, between Seventh and Eighth."

"Terrific." It was about as far out of her way as possible. "I have to make a stop first, at the store."

"What store?" He slipped an arm around her waist, as much for pleasure as to protect her from the cold.

"My store. We had the carpets laid today, and I didn't have time to check it before dinner. Since it's halfway between your place and mine, I might as well do it now."

"I didn't think business execs checked on carpet at nearly midnight."

"This one does." She smiled sweetly. "But if it's inconvenient for you, I'd be happy to drop you off at the bus stop."

"Thanks anyway." He waited while she unlocked her car. "Do you have any stock in that place yet?"

"About twenty percent of what we want for the grand opening. You're welcome to browse."

He slid into the car. "I was hoping you'd say that."

She drove well. That was no surprise. From what Ry had observed, Natalie Fletcher did everything with seamless competence. The fact that she could be shaken, the fact that the right word, the right look, at the right time, could bring a faint bloom to her cheeks, made her human. And outrageously appealing.

"Have you always lived in Urbana?" As she asked, she automatically turned down the radio.

"Yeah. I like it."

"So do I." She liked the movement of the city, the noise, the crowds. "We've had holdings here for years, of course, but I never lived in Urbana."

"Where?"

"Colorado Springs, mostly. That's where we're based, home and business. I like the East." The streets were dark now, and the wind was whipping through the canyons formed by the spearing buildings. "I like eastern cities, the way people live on top of each other and rush to get everywhere."

"No western comments about overcrowding and crime rates?"

"Fletcher Industries was founded on real estate, remember? The more people, the more housing required. And, as to crime…" She shrugged. "We have a hardworking police force. And Nemesis."

"You're interested in him."

"Who wouldn't be? Of course, as the sister of a police captain, I should add that I don't approve of private citizens doing police work."

"Why not? He seems to get the job done. I wouldn't mind having him on my side." He frowned as she stopped at a light. The streets were nearly empty here, with dark pockets and narrow alleys. "Do you do many runs like this alone?"

"When necessary."

"Why don't you have a driver?"

"Because I like to drive myself." She shot him a look just as the light turned green. "You're *not* going to be typical and give me a lecture about the dangers facing a woman alone in the city…."

"It's not all museums and French restaurants."

"Ry, I'm a big girl. I've spent time alone in Paris, Bangkok, London and Bonn, among other cities. I think I can handle Urbana."

"The cops, and your pal Nemesis, can't be everywhere," he pointed out.

"Any woman who has a big brother knows just how to drop a man to his knees," she said blithely. "And I've taken a self-defense course."

"That should make every mugger in the city tremble."

Ignoring the sarcasm, she pulled up to the curb and turned off the engine. "This is it."

The quick surge of pride rose the moment she

was out of the car and facing the building. Her building. "So, what do you think?"

It was sleek and feminine, like its owner. All marble and glass, and its wide display window was scrolled with the Lady's Choice logo in gold leaf. The entrance door was beveled glass etched with rosettes that glinted in the backwash from the streetlights.

Pretty, he thought. Impractical. Expensive.

"Nice look."

"As our flagship store, I wanted it to be impressive, classic, and…" She ran her fingertip over the etching. "Subtly erotic."

She dealt with the locks. Sturdy, Ry noted with some approval. Solid. Just inside the door, she paused to enter her code on the computerized security system. Natalie turned on the lights, relocked the front door.

"Perfect." She nodded with approval at the mauve carpet. The walls were teal, freshly painted. A curvy love seat and gleaming tea table were set in a corner to invite customers to relax and decide over merchandise.

Racks were recessed. Natalie could already envision them full, dripping with silks and laces in pastels, bold, vibrant colors and creamy whites.

"Most of the stock hasn't been put out yet. My manager and her staff will see to that this week. And the window treatment. We have the most incredible brocade peignoir. That'll be the focus."

Ry moved over to a faceless mannequin, fingered the lace at the leg of a jade teddy. The same color as Natalie's eyes, he thought. "So, what do you charge for something like this?"

"Mmm…" She examined the piece herself. Silk, seed pearls at the bodice. "Probably about one-fifty."

"One hundred and fifty? Dollars?" He shook his head in disgust. "One good tug and it's a rag."

Instantly she bristled. "Our merchandise is top-quality. It will certainly hold up to normal wear."

"Honey, a little number like this isn't designed for normal." He cocked a brow. "Looks about your size."

"You keep dreaming, Piasecki." She tossed her coat over the love seat. "The point of good lingerie is style, texture. The sheen of silk, the foam of lace. Ours is designed to make a woman feel attractive and good about herself—pampered."

"I thought the idea was to make a man beg."

"That couldn't hurt," she tossed back. "Look around, if you like. I'm going to run upstairs and check a couple of invoices while I'm here. It won't take me more than five minutes."

"I'll come with you. Offices upstairs?" he asked as they started toward a white floating staircase.

"Just the manager's. We'll have more merchandise up there, and changing rooms. We've also set up a separate area for brides. Specialized wedding-dress undergarments, honeymoon lingerie. Once we're fully operational—"

She broke off when he grabbed her arm. "Quiet."

"What—?"

"Quiet," he said again. He didn't hear it. Not yet. But he could smell it. Just the faintest sting in the air. "Do you have extinguishers in here?"

"Of course. In the storeroom, up in the office." She tugged at his hand. "What is this? Are you going to try to cite me for fire-code violations?"

"Get outside."

With her gaping after him, he darted toward the back of the store.

She was organized, he had to admit. He found the fire extinguisher, up to code, in full view in the crowded storeroom.

"What are you doing with that?" she demanded when he came back.

"I said get outside. You've got a fire."

"A—" He was halfway up the steps before she unfroze and raced after him. "That's impossible. How do you know? There's nothing—"

"Gas," he snapped out. "Smoke."

She started to tell him he was imagining things. But she smelled it now. "Ry…"

He cursed and kicked aside a streamer of papers and matches. It hadn't caught yet, but he saw where they were leading. The glossy white door was closed, and smoke was creeping sulkily under it.

He felt the door, and the heat pushing against it. His head whipped toward hers, the eyes cold. "Get out," he said again. "Call it in."

A scream strangled in her throat as he kicked the door open. Fire leapt out. Ry walked into it.

Chapter 5

It was like a dream. A nightmare. Standing there, frozen, while flame licked at the door frame and Ry stepped in to meet it. In the instant he disappeared into smoke and fire, her heart seemed to stop, its beat simply ceasing. Then the panic that had halted it whipped it to racing. Her head buzzed with the echo of a hundred pulses as she dashed to the door after him.

She could see him, smothering the fire that sprinted across the floor and ate merrily at the base of the walls. Smoke billowed around him, seared her eyes, burned her lungs. Like some warrior, he challenged it, fought it down. In horror, she saw it strike back and lick slyly at his arm.

Now she did scream, leaping in to pound at the smoke that puffed from his back. He whirled to face her, furious to find her there.

"You're on fire." She barely choked the words out. "For God's sake, Ry! Let it go."

"Stay back."

With an arching movement, he smothered the flames that had begun to lap at the central desk. The paperwork left on its top, he knew, would feed the fire. Focused, he turned to attack the smoldering baseboard, the intricately carved trim that was flaming.

"Take this." He shoved the extinguisher into her hands. The main fire was out, and the smaller ones were all but smothered. He nearly had it. From the terror in her eyes, he could see that she didn't realize the beast was nearly beaten. "Use it," he ordered, and in one stride he had reached the flaming curtains and torn them down. There would be pain later—he knew that, as well. But now he fought the fire hand to hand.

Once the smoldering, smoke-stained lace was nothing more than harmless rags, he snatched the extinguisher out of her numbed hands and killed what was left.

"It didn't have much of a start." But his jacket was still smoking. He yanked it off, tossed it aside. "Wouldn't have gotten this far this fast, if there weren't so many flammables in here." He set the nearly empty extinguisher aside. "It's out."

Still he checked the room, kicking through the ruined drapes, searching for any cagey spark that waited to burn clean again.

"It's out," he repeated, and shoved her toward the door. "Get downstairs."

She stumbled, almost falling to her knees. A violent fit of coughing nearly paralyzed her. Her stomach heaved, her head spun. Near fainting, she braced a hand against the wall and fought to breathe.

"Damn it, Natalie." In one sweep, he had her up in his arms. He carried her through the blinding smoke, down the elegant staircase. "I told you to get out. Don't you ever listen?"

She tried to speak, and only coughed weakly. It felt as though she were floating. Even when he laid her against the cool cushions of the love seat, her head continued to reel.

He was cursing her. But his voice seemed far

away, and harmless. If she could just get one breath, she thought, one full breath to soothe her burning throat.

He watched her eyes roll back. Jerking her ruthlessly, he pushed her head between her knees.

"Don't you faint on me." His voice was curt, his hand on the back of her head firm. "Stay here, breathe slow. You hear me?"

She nodded weakly. He left her, and when cold, fresh air slapped her cheeks, she shivered. After propping the outside door open, Ry came back, rubbing his hands up and down her spine.

She'd scared him, badly. So he did what came naturally to combat the fear—he yelled at her.

"That was stupid and thoughtless! You're lucky to get out of there with a sick stomach and some smoke inhalation. I *told* you to get out."

"You went in." She winced as the words tormented her abused throat. "You went right in."

"I'm trained. You're not." He hauled her back into a sitting position to check her over.

Her face was dead white under sooty smears, but her eyes were clear again. "Nausea?" he asked in clipped tones.

"No." She pressed the heels of her hands to her stinging eyes. "Not now."

"Dizzy?"

"No."

Her voice was hoarse, strained. He imagined her throat felt as though it had been scored with a hot poker. "Is there any water around here? I'll get you some."

"I'm all right." She dropped her hands, let her head fall back against the cushion. Now that the sickness was passing, fear was creeping in. "It seemed so fast, so horribly fast. Are you sure it's out?"

"It's my job to be sure." Frowning, he caught her chin, his eyes narrowing as he studied her face. "I'm taking you to the hospital."

"I don't need a damn hospital." In a bad-tempered movement, she shoved at him. Then gasped when she saw his hands. "Ry, your hands!" She grabbed his wrists. "You're burned!"

He glanced down. There were a few welts, some reddening. "Nothing major."

Reaction set in with shudders. "You were on fire, I saw your jacket catch fire."

"It was an old jacket. Stop," he ordered when tears swam in her eyes, overflowed. "Don't." If he hated one thing more than fire, it was a woman's tears. He swore and crushed his mouth to hers, hoping that would stop the flood.

Her arms came hard around him, surprising him with their strength and urgency. But her mouth trembled beneath his, moving him to gentle the kiss. To soothe.

"Better?" he murmured, and stroked her hair.

"I'm all right," she said again, willing herself to believe it. "There should be a first-aid kit in the storeroom. You need to put something on your hands."

"It's no big deal…." he began, but she shoved away from him and rose.

"I have to do something. Damn it, I have to do something."

She dashed off. Baffled by her, Ry stood and moved to relock the door. He needed to go up again and ventilate the office, but he wanted her out of the way before he made a preliminary investigation. He tugged off his tie, loosened his collar.

"There's some salve in here." Steadier now, Natalie came back in with a small first-aid kit.

"Fine." Deciding tending to him would do her some good, he sat back and let her play nurse. He had to admit the cool balm and her gentle fingers didn't do him any harm, either.

"You're lucky it isn't worse. It was insane, just walking into that room."

He cocked a brow. "You're welcome."

She looked up at him then. His face was smeared from the smoke, his eyes were reddened from it. "I am grateful," she said quietly. "Very grateful. But it was just things, Ry. Just things." She looked away again, busying herself replacing the tube of salve. "I guess I owe you a new suit."

"I hate suits." He shifted uncomfortably when he heard her quick, unsteady sob. "Don't cry again. If you really want to thank me, don't cry."

"All right." She sniffed inelegantly and rubbed her hands over her face. "I was so scared."

"It's over." He gave her hand an awkward pat. "Will you be all right for a minute? I want to go up and open the window. The smoke needs a way to escape."

"I'll come—"

"No, you won't. Sit here." He rose again, put a firm hand on her shoulder. "Please stay here."

He turned and left her. Natalie used the time he was gone to compose herself. And to think. When he came back down, she was sitting with her hands folded in her lap.

"It was the same as the warehouse, wasn't it?"

She lifted her gaze to his. "The way it was set. We can't pretend it was a coincidence."

"Yes," he said. "It was the same. And no, we can't. We'll talk about this later. I'll drive you home."

"I'm—"

The words slid back down her throat when he dragged her roughly to her feet. "If you tell me one more time that you're all right, I'm going to punch you. You're sick, you're scared, and you sucked in smoke. Now this is the way we're going to work this. I'm driving you home. We'll report this on the phone in that snazzy car of yours. You're going to go to bed, and tomorrow you're going to see a doctor. Once you check out, we'll go from there."

"Stop yelling at me."

"I wouldn't have to yell if you'd listen." He grabbed her coat. "Put this on."

"This is my property. I have a right to be here."

"Well, I'm taking you out." He shoved her arm into the sleeve of her coat. "If you don't like it, call your fancy lawyers and sue me."

"There's no reason for you to take this attitude."

He started to swear, stopped himself. As a precaution, he took one slow breath. "Natalie, I'm tired." His voice was quiet now, nearly reasonable. "I've got a job to do here, and I can't do it if you're in my way. So cooperate. Please."

He was right, she knew he was right. She turned away, picked up her purse. "Keep my car. I'll arrange to have it picked up tomorrow."

"I appreciate it."

She gave him the car keys and the keys to the shop. "I'll be here tomorrow, Ry."

"I figured you would." He lifted a hand and rubbed his knuckles along her jawline. "Hey—try not to worry. I'm the best."

She nearly smiled. "So I've been told."

It was nearly eight the following morning when the cab dropped Natalie off in front of Lady's Choice. She noted, without surprise, that her car was out front, a fire-department sign visible through the windshield.

Instead of bothering with the buzzer, she used the spare set of keys she'd picked up that morning at the office and let herself in.

She couldn't smell the smoke. That was a relief. She'd spent a great deal of time during the night worrying and calculating the possible losses if the stock already in place had been damaged by smoke.

The first floor looked as pristine and elegant as it had the night before. If Ry gave her the go-ahead, she'd contact her manager and reestablish business as usual.

She took off her coat and gloves and started upstairs.

For Ry, it had been a long and productive night. He'd stopped in at the station after he dropped Natalie off, to change and to pick up his tools. He'd worked alone through the night—the way he preferred it. He was just sealing an evidence jar when she walked in.

"Good morning, Legs." Crouched on the floor amid the rubble, he didn't bother to look past them.

She scanned the room, sighed. The carpet was a blackened mess. Charred pieces of wood trim had been pried from the sooty walls and lay scattered. The elegant Queen Anne desk was blackened and scored, and the Irish-lace drapes were a heap of useless rags.

Despite the open window where the light wind shook in thin snow, the air stank with stale smoke.

"Why does it always look worse the next day?"

"It's not so bad. A little paint, new trim."

She ran a fingertip over the wallpaper, the violet-and-rosebud pattern she'd chosen personally. Ruined now, she thought.

"Easy for you to say."

"Yeah," he agreed, labeling the evidence jar. "I guess it is."

He glanced up then. Today she'd scooped her hair up. The style appealed to him, the way it showed off the line of her neck and jaw. This morning's suit was royal purple, military in style. It looked, he thought, as though the lady were ready for a fight.

"How'd you sleep?"

"Surprisingly well, all in all." Except for one bone-chilling nightmare she didn't want to mention. "You?"

He hadn't been to bed at all, and merely shrugged. "Have you called your adjuster?"

"I will, as soon as his office opens." Her voice cooled automatically. "Are you going to interview me again, Inspector?"

Annoyance flared briefly in his eyes. "I don't think that's necessary, do you?" He began to replace his tools in their box. "I'll have a report by tomorrow."

She closed her eyes a moment. "I'm sorry. I'm not angry with you, Ry. I'm just angry."

"Fair enough."

"Can you—?" She broke off, turning quickly at the sound of footsteps on the stairs. "Gage." She forced a smile, held out her hands when he walked in.

"I heard." With one quick glance, he took in the damage. "I thought I'd come by and see if there was anything I could do."

"Thanks." She kissed him lightly on the cheek before she turned back to Ry. He was still crouched—very much, she thought, intrigued, like an animal about to spring. "Gage Guthrie, Inspector Ryan Piasecki."

"I've heard you do good work."

After a moment, Ry straightened and accepted the hand Gage offered. "I've heard the same about you." Feeling territorial, Ry measured the man as he spoke to Natalie. "Are you two pals?"

"That's right. And a bit more." She watched, fascinated, as Ry's eyes kindled. "If you can follow the connections, Gage is married to my brother's wife's sister."

The fire banked; Ry's shoulders relaxed. "Extended family."

"In a manner of speaking." Judging the situation quickly and accurately, Gage decided to do a little checking on the inspector himself. "Are you looking at the same fire starter here?"

"We're not ready to release that information."

"He's got his official hat on," Natalie said dryly. "Unofficially," she continued, ignoring Ry's scowl, "it looks the same. When we came in last night—"

"You were here?" Gage interrupted her, gripping Natalie's arm. "You?"

"I had a few things I wanted to check on. Fortunately." Blowing out a breath, she took another scan of the room. "It could have been a lot worse. I happened to have a veteran firefighter along."

Gage relaxed fractionally. "You've got no business going around the city alone, at night."

"Yeah." Ry took out a cigarette. "You try to tell her."

Natalie merely lifted a brow. "Do you go around the city, Gage, alone? At night?"

He tucked his tongue in his cheek. If she only knew. "It's entirely different. And don't give me a lecture on equality," he went on, before she could speak. "I'm all for it. In the home, in the workplace. But on the street it comes down to basic common sense. A woman's more of a target."

"Mmm, hmm…" Natalie smiled pleasantly. "And does Deborah buy that line from you?"

Now his lips did curve. "No. She's every bit as hardheaded as you." Frustrated that he'd been on the other side of town when Nat needed him, Gage tucked his hands in his pockets. "If I can't do anything else, I can offer you any of the facilities or staff of Guthrie International."

"I'll take you up on that if it becomes necessary." She sent him a quick, hopeful look. "I don't suppose you could use your influence to keep your wife from calling my brother and Cilla and relating all of this?"

He patted her cheek. "Not a chance. Maybe I should mention that she talked to Althea last week and filled her in on what happened at the warehouse."

Giving in to fatigue, Natalie rubbed her temples. Althea Grayson, her brother's former partner on the force, was very pregnant. "I'm surrounded by cops," she muttered. "There's no reason to get Althea upset in her condition. She and Colt should be concentrating on each other."

"It's a problem when you have so many people who care about you. Stay out of empty buildings," Gage added, and kissed her. "Nice to meet you, Inspector."

"Yeah. See you."

"Give Deborah and Addy my love," Natalie said as she walked Gage to the doorway. "And stop worrying about me."

"I'll do the first, but not the second."

"Who's Addy?" Ry asked before he heard the downstairs door close behind Gage.

"Hmmm? Oh, their baby." Distracted, she circled around a charred hole in the carpet to examine her antique filing cabinets. It was some consolation to see that they were undamaged. "I really need to clear this up, Ry. Too many people are losing sleep."

"You've got a lot of close ties." He walked to the open window and put out his cigarette. "I can't make this work any faster to please them. Just take your friend's advice. Stay off the streets at night and out of empty buildings."

"I don't want advice. I want answers. Someone broke in here last night and tried to burn me out. How and why?"

"Okay, Ms. Fletcher, I can give you the how." Ry leaned a hip against the partially burned desk. "On the night of February twenty-sixth, a fire was discovered by Inspector Piasecki, and Natalie Fletcher, owner of the building."

"Ry..."

He held up a hand to stop her. "After entering the building, Piasecki and Fletcher started up to the second floor when Piasecki detected the odor of an accelerant, and smoke. Piasecki then ordered Fletcher to flee the building. An order, I might add, that she stupidly ignored. Finding an extinguisher in the storeroom, Piasecki proceeded to the fire, which had involved an office on the second floor. Streamers of paper, clothing and matchbooks were observed. The fire was extinguished without extensive damage."

"I'm very aware of that particular sequence of events."

"You wanted a report, you're getting one. An examination of the debris led the investigator to believe that the fire had been started approximately two feet inside the door, with the use of gasoline as an accelerant. No forced entry into the building could be determined by the inspector, or the police department. Arson is indicated."

She took a careful breath. "You're angry with me."

"Yeah, I'm angry with you. You're pushing me, Natalie, and yourself. You want this all tidied up, because people are worried about you, and you're concerned with selling your pantyhose on time.

And you're missing one small, very important detail."

"No, I'm not." She was pale again, and rigid. "I'm trying not to be frightened by it. It isn't difficult to add the elements and come up with the fact that someone is doing this to me deliberately. Two of my buildings within two weeks. I'm not a fool, Ry."

"You're a fool if you're not frightened by it. You've got an enemy. Who?"

"I don't know," she shot back. "If I did, don't you think I'd tell you? You've just told me there was no forced entry. That means someone I know, someone who works for me, could have gotten in here and started the fire."

"It's a torch."

"Excuse me?"

"A pro," Ry explained. "Not a very good one, but a pro. Somebody hired a torch to set the fires. It could be that somebody let him in, or he found a way to bypass your security. But he didn't finish the job here, so it's likely he'll hit you again."

She forced back a shudder. "That's comforting. That's very comforting."

"I don't want you to be comforted. I want you to be alert. How many people work for you?"

"At Lady's Choice?" Frazzled, she pushed at her hair. "Around six hundred, I think, in Urbana."

"You got a personnel list?"

"I can get one."

"I want it. Look, I'm going to run the data through the computer. See how many known pros we have in the area who use this technique. It's a start."

"You'll keep me up-to-date? I'll be in the office most of the day. My assistant will know how to reach me if I'm out."

He straightened, walked to her and cupped her face. "Why don't you take the day off? Go shopping, go see a movie."

"Are you joking?"

He dropped his hands, shoved them in his pockets. "Listen, Natalie, you've got one more person worried about you. Okay?"

"I think it's okay," she said slowly. "I'll stay available, Ry. But I have a lot of work to do." She smiled in an attempt to lighten the mood. "Starting with getting a cleaning crew and decorators in here."

"Not until I tell you."

"How did I know you'd say that?" Resigned, she glanced toward the wooden cabinets against the left wall. "Is it all right if I get some files out? I only moved them out of the main office a few days ago so I could work on them here." She lifted a shoulder. "Or I'd hoped to work on them here. More delays," she said under her breath.

"Yeah, go ahead. Watch your step."

He watched it, as well, and shook his head. He didn't see how she could walk so smoothly on those skyscraper heels she seemed addicted to. But he had to admit, they did fascinating things to her legs.

"How are your hands?" she asked as she flipped through the files.

"What?"

"Your hands." She glanced back, saw where his gaze was focused, and laughed. "God, Piasecki, you're obsessed."

"I bet they go all the way up to your shoulders." He skimmed his eyes up to hers. "The hands aren't too bad, thanks. When's your doctor's appointment?"

She turned away to give unmerited attention to the files. "I don't need a doctor. I don't like doctors."

"Chicken."

"Maybe. My throat's a little sore, that's all. I

can deal with that without a doctor poking at me. And if you're going to lecture me on that, I'll lecture you on deliberately sucking smoke into your lungs."

With a wince, he tucked away the cigarette he'd just pulled out. "I didn't say anything. Are you about done? I want to get this evidence to the lab."

"Yes. The fact that the files didn't go up saves me a lot of time and trouble. I need Deirdre to run an audit after we've dealt with this other mess. I'm hoping things look solid enough for me to scout around and open a branch in Denver."

The little flutter under his heart wasn't easily ignored. "Denver? Are you going to be moving back to Colorado?"

"Hmmm…" Satisfied, she tucked the paperwork in her briefcase. "It depends. I'm not thinking that far ahead yet. First we have to get the stores we have off the ground. That isn't going to happen overnight." She swung the strap of her briefcase over her shoulder. "That should do it."

"I want to see you." It cost him to say it. Even more to admit it to himself. "I need to see you, Natalie. Away from all this."

Her suddenly nervous fingers tugged at the strap of her briefcase. "We're both pretty swamped at the moment, Ry. It might be smarter for us to concentrate on what needs to be done and keep a little personal distance."

"It would be smarter."

"Well, then." She took one step toward the door before he blocked her path.

"I want to see you," he repeated. "And I want to touch you. And I want to take you to bed."

Heat curled inside her, threatening to flash. It didn't seem to matter that his words were rough, blunt, and without finesse. Poetry and rose petals would have left her much less vulnerable.

"I know what you want. I need to be sure what *I* want. What I can handle. I've always been a logical person. You've got a way of clouding that."

"Tonight."

"I have to work late." She felt herself weakening, yearning. "A dinner meeting."

"I'll wait."

"I don't know when I'll be finished. Probably not much before midnight."

He backed her toward the wall. "Midnight, then."

She began to wonder why she was resisting. Her eyes started to cloud and close. "Midnight," she repeated, waiting for his mouth to cover hers. Wanting to taste it, to surge under it.

Her eyes sprang open. She jerked back. "Oh, God. Midnight."

Her cheeks had gone white again. Ry lifted his hands to support her. "What is it?"

"Midnight," she repeated, pressing a hand to her brow. "I didn't put it together. Never thought of it. It was just past twelve when we got here last night."

He nodded, watching her. "So?"

"I got a call when I was dressing for dinner. I never seem to be able to ignore the ring and let the machine pick up, so I answered. He said midnight."

Eyes narrowed, Ry braced her against the wall. "Who?"

"I don't know. I didn't recognize the voice. He said— Let me think." She pushed away to pace out into the hall. "Midnight. He said midnight. The witching hour. Watch for it, or wait for it—something like that." She gestured toward the charred and ruined carpet. "This must be what he meant."

"Why the hell didn't you tell me this before?"

"Because I just remembered." Every bit as angry as he, she whirled on Ry. "I thought it was a crank call, so I ignored it, forgot it. Then, when this happened, I had a little more on my mind than a nuisance call. How was I supposed to know it was a warning? Or a threat?"

He ignored that and took his notebook out of his pocket to write down the words she'd related. "What time did you get the call?"

"It must have been around seven-thirty. I was looking for earrings, and rushing because I'd gotten held up and was running late."

"Did you hear any background noises on the line?"

Unsure, she fought to remember. She hadn't been paying attention. She'd been thinking of Ry. "I didn't notice any. His voice was high-pitched. It was a man, I'm sure of that, but it was a girlish kind of voice. He giggled," she remembered.

Ry's gaze shot to her face, then back to his book. "Did it sound mechanical, or genuine?"

She went blank for a moment. "Oh, you mean like a tape. No, it didn't sound like a tape."

"Is your number listed?"

"No." Then she understood the significance of the question. "No," she repeated slowly. "It's not."

"I want a list of everyone who has your home number. Everyone."

She straightened, forcing herself to keep calm. "I can give you a list of everyone I know who has

it. I can't tell you who might have gotten it by
other means." She cleared her aching throat. "Ry,
do professionals usually call their victims before
a fire?"

He tucked his notebook away and looked into
her eyes. "Even pros can be crazy. I'll drive you
to your office."

"It's not necessary."

Patience. He reminded himself he'd worked overtime so that he could be patient with her. Then he
thought, the hell with it. "You listen to this, real
careful." He curled his fingers around the lapel of her
jacket. "I'm driving you to your office. Got that?"

"I don't see—"

He tugged. "Got it?"

She bit back an oath. It would be petty to argue.
"Fine. I'm going to need my car later today, so
you'll have to get yourself wherever you're going
after you drop me off."

"Keep listening," he said evenly. "Until I get
back to you, you're not to go anywhere alone."

"That's ridiculous. I've got a business to run."

"Nowhere alone," he repeated. "Otherwise, I'm
going to call some of my pals in Urbana P.D. and
have them sit on you." When she opened her
mouth to protest, he overrode her. "And I can sure

as hell keep your little shop here off-limits to everyone but official fire- and police-department personnel until further notice."

"That sounds like a threat," she said stiffly.

"You're a real sharp lady. You get one of your minions to drive you today, Natalie, or I'll slap a fire-department restriction on the front door of this place for the next couple of weeks."

He could, she realized, reading the determination on his face. And he would. From experience, she knew it was smarter, and more practical, to give up a small point in a negotiation in order to salvage the bottom line.

"All right. I'll assign a driver for any out-of-the-office meetings today. But I'd like to point out that this man is burning my buildings, Ry, not threatening me personally."

"He called you personally. That's enough."

She hated the fact that he'd frightened her. Stringent control kept her dealing with office details coolly, efficiently. By noon, she had a cleanup crew on standby, waiting for Ry's okay. She'd ordered her assistant to contact the decorator about new carpet, wallpaper, draperies and paint. She'd dealt with a frantic call from her Atlanta branch and an irate one from Chicago, and managed to play down the problem with her family back in Colorado.

Impatient, she buzzed her assistant. "Maureen, I needed those printouts thirty minutes ago."

"Yes, Ms. Fletcher. The system's down in Accounting. They're working on it."

"Tell them—" She bit back the searing words, and forced her voice to level. "Tell them it's a priority. Thank you, Maureen."

Deliberately she leaned back in her chair and closed her eyes. Having an edge was an advantage in business, she reminded herself. Being edgy was a liability. If she was going to handle the meetings set for the rest of the day, she had to pull herself together. Slowly she unfisted her hands and ordered her muscles to relax.

She'd nearly accomplished it when a quick knock came at her door. She straightened in her chair as Melvin poked his head in.

"Safe?"

"Nearly," she told him. "Come in."

"I come bearing gifts." He carried a tray into the room.

"If that's coffee, I may find the energy to get up and kiss your whole face."

He flushed brightly and chuckled. "Not only is it coffee, but there's chicken salad to go with it. Even *you* have to eat, Natalie."

"Tell me about it." She pressed a hand to her stomach as she rose to join him at the sofa. "I'm empty. This is very sweet of you, Melvin."

"And self-serving. You've been burning up the interoffice lines, so I had my secretary put this together. You take a break—" he fiddled with his bright red bow tie "—we take a break."

"I guess I have been playing Simon Legree today." With a little sigh, Natalie inhaled the scent of coffee as she poured.

"You're entitled." He sat beside her. "Have you got time over lunch to tell me how bad things are over at the flagship?"

"Not as bad as they could have been." She indulged herself by slipping out of her shoes and tucking her legs up as she ate. "Minor, really. From what I could tell, it looked like mostly cosmetic damage to the manager's office. It didn't get to the stock."

"Thank God," he said heartily. "I don't know how much my charm would have worked a second time in persuading the branches to part with inventory."

"Unnecessary," she said between bites. "We got lucky this time, Melvin, but—"

"But?"

"There's a pattern here that concerns me. Someone doesn't want Lady's Choice to fly."

Frowning, he picked up the roll on her plate, broke it in half. "Unforgettable Woman's our top competitor. Or we'll be theirs."

"I've thought of that. It just doesn't fit. That company's been around nearly fifty years. It's solid. Respectable." She sighed, hating what she needed to say. "But I am worried about corporate espionage, Melvin. Within Lady's Choice."

"One of our people?" He'd lost his taste for the roll.

"It isn't a possibility I like—or one I can overlook." Thoughtful, she switched from food to coffee. "I could call a meeting of department heads, get input and opinions about their people." And she would, she thought. She would have to. "But that doesn't deal with the department heads themselves."

"A lot of your top people have been with Fletcher for years, Natalie."

"I'm aware of that." Restless, she rose, drinking coffee as she paced. "I can't think of any reason why someone in the organization would want to delay the opening. But I have to look for that reason."

"That puts us all under the gun."

She turned back. "I'm sorry, Melvin. It does."

"No need to be sorry. It's business." He waved it aside, but his smile was a little strained as he rose. "What's the next step?"

"I'm going to meet the adjuster at the shop at one." She glanced at her watch and swore. "I'd better get started."

"Let me do it." Anticipating her, Melvin held up a hand. "You have more than you can handle right here. Delegate, Natalie, remember? I'll meet the agent, give you a full report when I get back."

"All right. It would save me a very frenzied hour." Frowning, she stepped back into her shoes. "If the arson inspector is on-site, you might ask him to contact me with any progress."

"Will do. There's a shipment due in to the shop late this afternoon. Do you want to put a hold on it?"

"No." She'd already thought it through. "Business as usual. I've put a security guard on the building. It won't be easy for anyone to get in again."

"We'll stay on schedule," Melvin assured her.

"Damn right we will."

Chapter 6

Ry preferred good solid human reasoning to computer analysis, but he'd learned to use all available tools. The Arson Pattern Recognition System was one of the best. Over the past few years, he'd become adept enough at the keyboard. Now, with his secretary long gone for the day and the men downstairs settled into sleep, he worked alone.

The APRS, used intelligently, was an effective tool for identifying and classifying trends in data. It was possible, with a series of fires suspected to be related, to use the tool to predict where and when future arsons in the series were most likely to occur.

The computer told him what he'd already deduced. Natalie's production plant was a prime target. He'd already assigned a team to patrol and survey the area.

But he was more concerned about Natalie herself. The phone call she'd received made it personal. And it had given him a very specific clue.

Reaching for coffee with one hand, Ry tapped on keys and linked up with the National Fire Data System. He plugged in his pattern—incident information, geographical locations and fire data. The process would not only help him, but serve to aid future investigators.

Then he worked on suspects. Again he input the fire data, the method. To these he was able to add the phone call, Natalie's impression of the voice and the wording.

He sat back and watched the computer reinforce his own conclusions.

Clarence Robert Jacoby, a.k.a. Jacoby, a.k.a. Clarence Roberts. Last known address 23 South Street, Urbana. White male. D.O.B. 6/25/52.

It went on to list half a dozen arrests for arson and incendiary fires, all urban. One conviction had put him away for five years. Another arrest, two years ago was still pending, as he'd skipped out on bail.

And the pattern was there.

Jacoby was a part-time pro who liked to burn things. He habitually preferred gasoline as an accelerant, used streamers of convenient, on-site flammables, along with matchbooks from his own collection. He often called his victims. His psychiatric evaluation classified him as a neurotic with sociopathic tendencies.

"You like fire, don't you, you little bastard?" Ry muttered, tapping his finger against the keyboard. "You don't even mind when it burns you. Isn't that what you told me? It's like a kiss."

Ry flipped a switch and had the data printing out. Wearily he rubbed the heels of his hands over his eyes as the machine clattered. He'd caught about two hours' sleep on the sofa in the outer office that evening. Fatigue was catching up with him.

But he had his quarry now. He was sure of it. And, he thought, he had a trail.

More out of habit than desire, Ry lit a cigarette before punching in numbers on the phone. "Piasecki. I'm swinging by the Fletcher plant on my way home. You can reach me…" He trailed off, checking his watch. Midnight, he noted. On the dot. Maybe he should take that as a sign. "You can reach me at this number until I check in again." He recited Natalie's home number from memory, then hung up.

He shut down the computer, grabbed the print-out and his jacket, then hit the lights.

Natalie pulled on a robe, one of her favorites from the Lady's Choice line, and debated whether to crawl into bed or sink into a hot bath. She decided to soothe her nerves with a glass of wine before she did either. She'd tried to reach Ry three times that afternoon, only to be told he was un-available.

She was supposed to be available, she thought nastily. But he could come and go as he pleased. Not a word all day. Well, he was going to get a sur-prise first thing in the morning when she walked right into his office and demanded a progress re-port.

As if she didn't have enough to worry about, with department meetings, production meetings, meeting meetings. And she was tracking the early catalog orders by region. At least that looked promising, she thought, and walked over to enjoy her view of the city.

She wasn't going to let anything stand in her way. Not fires, and certainly not a fire inspector. If there was someone on her staff—in any position—who was responsible for the arson, she would find out who it was. And she would deal with it.

Within a year, she would have pushed Lady's Choice over the top. Within five, she would double the number of branches.

Fletcher Industries would have a new success, one she would have nurtured from inception. She could be proud, and satisfied.

So why was she suddenly so lonely?

His fault, she decided, sipping her wine, for making her restless with her life. For making her question her priorities at a time when she needed all her concentration and effort focused.

Physical attraction, even with this kind of intensity, wasn't enough, shouldn't be enough, to distract her from her goals. She'd been attracted before, and certainly knew how to play the game safely. After all, she was thirty-two, hardly a novice in the relationship arena. Skilled and cautious, she'd always come through unscathed. No man had ever involved her heart quite enough to cause scarring.

Why did that suddenly seem so sad?

Annoyed with the thought, she shook it off.

She was wasting her time brooding about Ryan Piasecki. God knew, he wasn't even her type. He was rough and rude and undeniably abrasive. She preferred a smoother sort. A safer sort.

Why did that suddenly seem so shallow?

She set her half-full glass aside and shook back her hair. What she needed was sleep, not self-analysis. The phone rang just as she reached out to switch off the lights.

"Oh, I hate you," she muttered, and picked up the receiver. "Hello."

"Ms. Fletcher, this is Mark, at the desk downstairs?"

"Yes, Mark, what is it?"

"There's an Inspector Piasecki here to see you."

"Oh, really?" She checked her watch, toying with the idea of sending him away. "Mark, would you ask him if it's official business?"

"Yes, ma'am. Is this official business, Inspector?"

She heard Ry's voice clearly through the earpiece, asking Mark whether he would like him to get a team down there in the next twenty minutes to look for code violations.

When Mark sputtered, Natalie took pity on him. "Just send him up, Mark."

"Yes, Ms. Fletcher. Thank you."

She disconnected, then paced to the door and back. She certainly wasn't going to check her appearance in the mirror.

Of course, she did.

By the time Ry pounded on her door, she'd managed to dash into the bedroom, brush her hair and dab on some perfume.

"Don't you think it's unfair to threaten people in order to get your way?" she demanded when she yanked open the door.

"Not when it works." He took his time looking at her. The floor-length robe was unadorned, the color of heavy cream. The silk crossed over her breasts, nipped in at the belted waist, then fell, thin and close, down her hips.

"Don't you think it's a waste to wear something like that when you're alone?"

"No, I don't."

"Are we going to talk in the hall?"

"I suppose not." She closed the door behind him. "I won't bother to point out that it's late."

He said nothing, only wandered around the living area of the apartment. Soft colors, offset by those vibrant abstract paintings she apparently liked. Lots of trinkets, he noted, but tidy. There were fresh flowers, a fireplace piped for gas, and a wide window through which the lights of the city gleamed.

"Nice place."

"I like it."

"You like heights." He moved to the window and looked down. She was a good twenty floors above any possible ladder rescue. "Maybe I will have this place checked to see if it's up to code." He glanced back at her. "Got a beer?"

"No." Then she sighed. Manners would always rise above annoyance. "I was having a glass of wine. Would you like one?"

He shrugged. He wasn't much of a wine drinker, but his system couldn't handle any more coffee.

Taking that as an indication of assent, Natalie went into the kitchen to pour another glass.

"Got anything to go with it?" he asked from the doorway. "Like food?"

She started to snap at him about mistaking her apartment for an all-night diner, but then she got a good look at his face in the strong kitchen light. If she'd ever seen exhaustion, she was seeing it now.

"I don't do a lot of cooking, but I have some Brie, crackers, some fruit."

Nearly amused, he rubbed his hands over his face. "Brie." He gave a short laugh as he dropped his hands. "Great. Fine."

"Go sit down." She handed him the wine. "I'll bring it out."

"Thanks."

A few minutes later, she found him on her sofa, his legs stretched out, his eyes half-closed. "Why aren't you home in bed?"

"I had some stuff to do." With one hand, he reached for the tray she'd set on the table. With the other, he reached for her. Content with her beside him, he piled soft cheese on a cracker. "It's not half-bad," he said with his mouth full. "I missed dinner."

"I suppose I could send out for something."

"This is fine. I figured you'd want an update."

"I do, but I thought I'd hear from you several hours ago." He mumbled something over a new cracker. "What?"

"Court," he said, and swallowed. "I had to be in court most of the afternoon."

"I see."

"Got your messages, though." The refueling helped, and he grinned. "Did you miss me?"

"The update," she said dryly. "It's the least you can do while you're cleaning out my pantry."

He helped himself to a handful of glossy green grapes. "I've ordered surveillance for your plant on Winesap."

Her fingers tightened on the stem of her glass. "Do you think it's a target?"

"Fits the pattern. Have you noticed a man around any of your properties? White guy, about five-four, a hundred and thirty. Thinning sandy hair. Fifty-something, but with this round, moony face that makes him look like a kid." He broke off to wash crackers down with wine. "Pale, mousy-looking eyes, lots of teeth."

"No, I can't think of anyone like that. Why?"

"He's a torch. Nasty little guy, about half-crazy." The wine wasn't half-bad, either, Ry was discovering, and sipped again. "All-the-way crazy would be easier. He likes to make things burn, and he doesn't mind getting paid for it."

"You think he's the one," Natalie said quietly. "And you know him, personally, don't you?"

"We've met, Clarence and me. Last time I saw

him was, oh, about ten years ago. He'd hung around too long on one of his jobs. He was on fire when I got to him. We were both smoking by the time I got him out."

Natalie struggled for calm. "Why do you think it's him?"

Briefly Ry gave her a rundown on his work that evening. "So, it's his kind of job," he added. "Plus, the phone call. He likes the phone, too. And the voice you described—that's pure Clarence."

"You could have told me that this morning."

"Could've." He shrugged. "Didn't see the point."

"The point," she said between her teeth, "is that we're talking about my building, my property."

He studied her a moment. It wasn't such a bad idea, he supposed, to use anger to cover fear. He couldn't blame her for it. "Tell me, Ms. Fletcher, in your position as CEO, or whatever it is you are, do you make reports before, during, or after you've checked your data?"

It irritated, as he'd meant it to. And it deflated. As he'd meant it to. "All right." She expelled a rush of air. "Tell me the rest."

Ry set his glass aside. "He moves around, city to city. I'm betting he's back in Urbana. And I'll find him. Is there an ashtray around here?"

In silence, Natalie rose and took a small mosaic dish from another table. She was being unfair, she realized, and it wasn't like her. Obviously he was dead tired because he'd put in dozens of extra hours—for her.

"You've been working on this all night."

He struck a match. "That's the job."

"Is it?" she asked quietly.

"Yeah." His eyes met hers. "And it's you."

Her pulse began to drum. She couldn't stop it. "You're making it very hard for me, Ry."

"That's the idea." Lazily he skimmed a finger along the lapel of her robe, barely brushing the skin. Her scent rose up from it, subtly, tantalizingly. "You want me to ask you how your day went?"

"No." With a tired laugh, she shook her head. "No."

"I guess you don't want to talk about the weather, politics, sports?"

Natalie paused before she spoke again. She didn't want her voice to sound breathy. "Not particularly."

He grunted, leaned over to crush out his cigarette. "I should go, let you get some sleep."

Her emotions tangled, she rose as he did. "That's probably best. Sensible." It wasn't what she wanted, just what was best. And it wasn't, she'd begun to realize, what she needed. Just what was sensible.

"But I'm not going to." His eyes locked on hers. "Unless you tell me."

Her heartbeat thickened. She could feel the shudder start all the way down in the soles of her feet and work its way up. "Tell you what?"

He smiled, moved closer, stopping just before their bodies brushed. The first answer, whether she wanted him to go or stay, was already easily read in her eyes.

"Where's the bedroom, Natalie?"

A little dazed, she looked over his shoulder, gesturing vaguely. "There. Back there."

With that quick, surprising grace of his, he scooped her up. "I think I can make it that far."

"This is a mistake." She was already raining kisses over his face, his throat. "I know it's a mistake."

"Everybody makes one now and again."

"I'm smart." While her breath hitched, her fingers hurried to unbutton his shirt. "And I'm level-headed. I have to be, because…" She let out a groan as her fingers found flesh. "God, I love your body."

"Yeah?" He nearly staggered as she tugged his

shirt out of his jeans. "Consider it all yours. I should have known."

"Mmm…" She was busy biting at his shoulder. "What?"

"That you'd have a first-class bed." He tumbled with her onto the satin covers.

Already half-mad for him, she dragged at his shirt. "Hurry," she demanded. "I've wanted you to hurry since the first time you touched me."

"Let me catch up." Equally frantic, he crushed his mouth to hers, sinking in.

Breathless, she yanked at the snap of his jeans. "This is insane." She struggled to find him, drinking hungrily from his mouth as they rolled across the bed.

He couldn't catch his breath, or even a slippery hold on control. "It's about to be," he muttered. Tugging her robe open, he found the thin swatch of matching silk beneath. A moan ripped through him as he closed his mouth over her cream-covered breast.

Silk and heat and fragrant flesh. Everything she was filled him, taunted him, tormented him. Woman, all woman. Beauty and grace and passion. Temptation and torment and triumph. All of it, all of her, obsessed him.

They thrashed over the slick satin spread, groping for more.

Here was fire, the bright, dangerous flash of it. It seared through him, burned, scarred, while her hands and mouth raced over him, igniting hundreds of new flames. He didn't fight it back. For once he wanted to be consumed. With an oath, he tore at the silk and dined greedily on her flesh.

His hands were rough and hard. And wonderful. She'd never felt more alive, or more desperate. She craved him, knew that she had, on some deep level, right from the beginning.

But now she had him, could feel the press of that hard, muscled body against her, could taste the violent urgency of his need whenever their mouths met, could hear his response to her touch, to her taste, in every hurried breath.

If it was elemental, so be it. She felt lusty and wanton and absolutely free. Her teeth dug into his shoulder as he whipped her ruthlessly over the first crest. She cried out his name, all but screamed it, arching upward, taut as a bow.

He arrowed into her, hard, deep.

She was blind and deaf from the pleasure of it, oblivious of her own sobbing breaths as they mated in a frenzied rhythm. Her body plunged against his, tireless, driven by a need that seemed insatiable.

Then body and need erupted.

The light was on. Funny he hadn't even noticed that, when normally he was accustomed to picking up every small detail. The lamp's glow was soft, picking up the cool sherbet tones of her bedroom.

Ryan lay still, his head on her breast, and waited for his system to level. Beneath his ear, her heart continued to thunder. Her flesh was damp, her body limp. Every few moments a tremor shook her.

He didn't smile in triumph, as he might have done, but simply stared in wonder.

He'd wanted to conquer her. He couldn't—wouldn't—deny it. He'd craved the sensation of having her body buck and shudder under his from the first moment he saw her.

But he hadn't expected the tornado of need that had swept through them both, that had them clawing at each other like animals.

He knew he'd been rough. He wasn't a particularly gentle man, so that didn't bother him. But he'd never lost control so completely with any woman. Nor had he ever wanted one so intensely only moments after he'd had her.

"That should have done it," he muttered.

"Hmmm?" She felt weak as water. Achy and sweet.

"It should have gotten it out of my system. Gotten *you* out. At least started getting you out."

"Oh." She found the energy to open her eyes. The light, dim as it was, had her wincing. Slowly, her mind began to clear; quickly, her skin began to heat. She remembered the way she'd torn at his clothes, wrestled him into bed without a single coherent thought except having him.

She let out a breath, drew another in.

"You're right," she decided. "It should have. What's wrong with us?"

With a laugh, he lifted his head, looking at her flushed face, her tousled hair. "Damned if I know. Are you okay?"

Now she smiled. The hell with logic. "Damned if I know. What just happened here's a bit out of the usual realm for me."

"Good." He lowered his head, skimmed his tongue lightly over her breast. "I want you again, Natalie."

She quivered once. "Good."

* * *

When the alarm went off, Natalie groaned, rolled over to shut it off, and bumped solidly into Ry. He grunted, slapped at the buzzer with one hand and brought her to rest on top of him with the other.

"What's the noise for?" he asked, and ran an interested hand down her spine to the hip.

"To wake me up."

He opened one eye. Yeah, he thought, he should have known it. She looked just as good in the morning as she did every other time of the day. "Why?"

"It goes like this." Still groggy, she pushed her hair out of her face. "The alarm goes off, I get up, shower, dress, drink copious cups of coffee, and go to work."

"I've had some experience with the process. Anybody tell you today's Saturday?"

"I know what day it is," she said. At least she did now. "I have work."

"No, you don't, you just think you do." He cradled her head against his shoulder, casting one bleary eye at the clock. It was 7:00 a.m. He calculated they'd had three hours' sleep, at the outside. "Go back to sleep."

"I can't."

He let out a long-suffering sigh. "All right, all right. But you should have warned me you were insatiable." More than willing to oblige, he rolled her over again and began to nibble on her shoulder.

"I didn't mean that." She laughed, trying to wiggle free. "I have paperwork, calls to make." His hand was sneaking up to stroke her breast. Fire kindled instantly in the pit of her stomach. "Cut it out."

"Uh-uh. You woke me up, now you pay."

She couldn't help it, simply couldn't, and she began to stretch under his hands. "We're lucky we didn't kill each other last night. Are you sure you want to take another chance?"

"Men like me face danger every day." He covered her grinning mouth with his.

She was more than three hours behind schedule when she stepped out of the shower. So, she'd work late, Natalie decided, and after wrapping a towel around her hair she began to cream her legs. A good executive understood the merits of flextime.

Yawning, she wiped steam from the bathroom

mirror and took a good look at her face. She should be exhausted, she realized. She certainly should look exhausted after the wild night she and Ry had shared.

But she wasn't. And she didn't. She looked... soft, she thought. Satisfied.

And why not? she thought, dragging the towel from her hair. When a woman took thirty-two years to experience just what a bout of hot, sweaty sex could do for the mind and body, she ought to look satisfied.

Nothing, absolutely nothing, she'd ever experienced, came close to what she'd felt, what she'd done, what she'd discovered, during the night with Ry.

So if she smiled like a fool while she combed out her wet hair, why not? If she felt like singing as she wrapped her tingling body in her robe, it was understandable.

And if she had to rearrange her schedule for the day because she'd spent most of the night and all of the morning wrestling in bed with a man who made her blood bubble, more power to her.

She stepped back into the bedroom and grinned at the tangled sheets. Lips pursed, she picked up the remains of her chemise. The strap was torn, and a froth of lace hung limp. Apparently, she decided, her merchandise didn't quite live up to Ry Piasecki's idea of wear and tear.

And wasn't it fabulous?

Laughing out loud, she tossed the chemise aside and followed her nose into the kitchen.

"I smell coffee," she began, then paused in the doorway.

He was breaking eggs into a bowl with those big, hard hands of his. His hair was damp, as hers was, because he'd beaten her to the shower. He was barefoot, jeans snug at his hips, flannel shirt rolled up to the elbows.

Incredibly, she wanted him all over again.

"You have next to nothing in this place to eat."

"I eat out a lot." With an order to control herself, she moved to the coffeepot. "What are you making?"

"Omelets. You had four eggs, some cheddar and some very limp broccoli."

"I was going to steam it." She cocked her head as she sampled the coffee. "So you cook."

"Every self-respecting firefighter cooks. You take shifts at the station." He located a whisk, then turned to her. Wet hair, glowing face, sleepy eyes. "Hello, Legs. You look good."

"Thanks." She smiled over the rim of her cup. If he continued to look at her in just that way, she realized, she would drag him right down onto the floor. It might be wise, she decided, to tend to some practical matters. "Am I supposed to help?"

"Can you handle toast?"

"Barely." She set her cup aside and opened the cupboard. They worked in silence for a moment, he beating eggs, she popping bread in the toaster. "I…" She wasn't sure how to put it, delicately. "I suppose when you were fighting fires, you faced a lot of dangerous situations."

"Yeah. So?"

"The scars on your shoulder, your back." She'd discovered them in her explorations in the night, the raised welts and scarred ridges over that taut, really beautiful body. "Line of duty?"

"That's right." He glanced up. In truth, he didn't think about them. But it occurred to him in the harsh light of day that a woman like her might find them offensive. "Do they bother you?"

"No. I just wondered how you got burned."

He set the bowl aside and placed a pan on the stove to heat. Maybe they bothered her, he thought, maybe they didn't. But it seemed best to get the matter out of the way.

"Our friend Clarence. While I was pulling him out of the fire he started, the ceiling collapsed." Ry could remember it still, the rain of flame, the animal roar of it, the staggering nightmare of pain. "It fell down on us like judgment. He was screaming, laughing. I got him outside. I don't remember much after that, until I woke up in the burn ward."

"I'm sorry."

"It could have been a lot worse. My gear went a long way toward protecting me. I got off lucky." Deliberately focused, he poured the beaten eggs into the pan. "My father went down like that. Fire went into the walls. When they ventilated the ceiling, it went. It all went."

He cursed under his breath. Where the hell had that come from? he wondered. He hadn't meant to say it. The death of his father certainly wasn't typical morning-after conversation.

"You should butter that toast before it gets cold."

She said nothing, could think of nothing, only went to him, wrapping her arms around his waist, pressing her cheek to his back.

"I didn't know you'd lost your father." There was so much, she thought, that she didn't know.

"Twelve years ago. It was in a high school. Some kid who wasn't happy with his chemistry grade torched the lab. It got away from him. Pop knew the risks," he muttered, uncomfortable with the sensation her quiet sympathy was stirring. "We all know them."

She held on. "I didn't mean to open old wounds, Ry."

"It's all right. He was a hell of a smoke eater."

Natalie stayed where she was another moment, baffled by what she was feeling. This need to comfort, to share, this terrible urge to be part of what he was. Cautious, she stepped back. It wouldn't do, she reminded herself. It wouldn't do at all to look for more between them than what there was.

"And this Clarence—how will you find him?"

"I could get lucky and track him down through contacts." With a quick, competent touch, Ry folded the egg mixture. "Or we'll pick him up when he scouts out his next target."

"My plant."

"Probably." More relaxed now that there was a little distance between them, he shot her a look over his shoulder. "Cheer up, Natalie. You've got the best in the city working to protect your nighties."

"You know very well it's not just—" She broke off when her doorbell rang. "Never mind."

"Hold on. Doesn't your doorman call up when someone's coming to see you?"

"Not if it's a neighbor."

"Use the judas hole," he ordered, and reached for plates.

"Yes, Daddy." Amused by him, Natalie went to the door. One look through the peephole had her stifling a shout and dragging back the locks. "Boyd, for heaven's sake!" She threw her arms around her brother. "Cilla!"

"The whole crew," Cilla warned her, laughing as they hugged. "The cop wouldn't let me call ahead and alert you to the invasion."

"I'm just so glad to see you." She bent down to hug her niece and nephews. "But what are you doing here?"

"Checking up on you." Boyd shifted the bag of take-out he carried to his other hip.

"You know the captain," Cilla said. "Bryant, touch nothing under penalty of death." She aimed a cautious look at her oldest son. At eight, he couldn't be trusted. "The minute Deborah called us about the second fire, he herded us up and moved us out. Allison, this isn't a basketball court. Why don't you put that down now?"

Territorial, Allison hugged the basketball to her chest. "I'm not going to throw it or anything."

"She's fine," Natalie assured Cilla, stroking a distracted hand down Allison's golden hair. "Boyd, I can't believe you'd drag everyone across the country for something like this."

"The kids have Monday off at school." Boyd crouched down to pick up the jacket their youngest had already tossed on the floor. "So we're taking a quick weekend, that's all."

"We're staying with Deborah and Gage," Cilla added. "So don't panic."

"It's not that…"

"And we brought supplies." Boyd held out the bag filled with take-out burgers and fries. "How about lunch?"

"Well, I…" She cleared her throat and looked toward the kitchen. How, she wondered, was she going to explain Ry?

Keenan, with the curiosity of an active five-year-old, had already discovered him. From the kitchen doorway, he grinned up at Ry. "Hi."

"Hi yourself." Curious to see just how Natalie handled things, Ry strolled out of the kitchen.

"Want to see what I can do?" Keenan asked him before anyone else could speak.

"Sure."

Always ready to show off a new skill, Keenan

shimmied up Ry's leg, scooting up and around until he was riding piggy-back.

"Not bad." Ry gave the boy a little boost to settle him in place.

"That's Keenan," Cilla explained, running her tongue over her teeth as she considered. "Our youngest monkey."

"I'm sorry. Ah…" Natalie dragged a hand through her damp hair. She didn't have to look at Boyd to know he'd have that speculative big-brother look in his eyes. "Boyd and Cilla Fletcher, Ry Piasecki." She cleared her throat. "And this is Allison, and Bryant." Now she sighed. "You've already met Keenan."

"Piasecki," Boyd repeated. "Arson?" Just the man he wanted to see, Boyd thought. But he hadn't expected to find him barefoot in his sister's kitchen.

"That's right." Brother and sister shared strong good looks, Ry mused. And, he thought, an innate suspicion of strangers. "You're the cop from Denver."

Bryant piped up. "He's a police captain. He wears a gun to work. Can I have a drink, Aunt Nat?"

"Sure. I—" But Bryant was already darting into the kitchen. "Well, this is…" Awkward, she thought. "Maybe I should get some plates before the food gets cold."

"Good idea. All she has is eggs." Ry eyed the bag Boyd still carried, recognizing the package. "Maybe we can work a deal for some of your french fries."

"You're the one investigating the fires, right?" Boyd began.

"Slick," Cilla said, glaring at her husband. "No interrogations on an empty stomach. You can grill him after we eat. We've been on a plane for hours," she explained when Bryant came back in and tried to wrestle the ball away from Allison. "We're a little edgy."

"No problem." An instant before Boyd, Ry snatched the ball that squirted out of flailing hands. "Like to shoot hoop?" he asked Allison.

"Uh-huh." She gave him a quick, winning smile. "I made the team. Bryant didn't."

"Basketball's stupid." Sulking, Bryant slouched in a chair. "I'd rather play Nintendo."

Ry juggled Keenan on his back as he turned the ball in his hands. "It so happens I've got a game in a couple of hours. Maybe you'd like to come."

"Really?" Allison's eyes lit as she turned to Cilla. "Mom?"

"It sounds like fun." Intrigued, Cilla strolled toward the kitchen. "I'll just give Natalie a hand."

And, she thought, pump her sister-in-law for details.

Chapter 7

The last place Natalie expected to spend her Saturday afternoon was courtside, watching cops and firefighters play round ball. She sulked through most of the first quarter, her elbow on her knee, her chin on her fist.

After all, Ry hadn't mentioned the game to her, hadn't directly invited her. She was there to witness what was obviously an important annual rivalry only because of her niece.

Not that it mattered to her, she assured herself. Ry was certainly under no obligation to include her in his personal entertainment.

The pig.

Beside her, Allison was in basketball heaven, cheering on the red jerseys with a rabid fan's passionate enthusiasm. Her brandy-colored eyes glinted as she followed the action up and down the court of the old west-side gym.

"It's not such a bad way to spend the afternoon," Cilla commented over the shrill sound of the ref's whistle. "Watching a bunch of half-naked guys sweat." Her eyes, the same warm shade as her daughter's, danced. "By the way, your guy's very cute."

"I told you, he's not my guy. We're just…"

"Yeah, you told me." Chuckling, Cilla wrapped an arm around Natalie's shoulders. "Cheer up, Nat. If you'd gone along with Boyd and the boys to unload at Deborah's, your big bro would be grilling you right now."

"You've got a point." She let out a sigh. Despite herself, she was following the action. The cops were double-teaming Ry consistently, she noted. Not a bad strategy, as he played like a steamroller, and had already scored seven points in the first quarter.

Not that she was counting.

"He didn't mention this game to me," she muttered.

"Oh?" Fighting back a grin, Cilla ran her tongue over her teeth. "He must have had something else on his mind. Hey!" She surged to her feet, along with most of the crowd, as one of the blue jerseys rammed an elbow sharply in Ry's ribs. "Foul!" Cilla shouted between her cupped hands.

"He can take it," Natalie mumbled, and tried not to care as Ry approached the foul line. "He's got an iron stomach." She struggled between pride and resentment when he sank his shot.

"Ry's the best." Allison beamed, well into a deep case of hero worship. "Did you see how he moves up-court? And he's got a terrific vertical leap. He's already blocked three shots under the hoop."

So, maybe he looked good, Natalie conceded. Those long, muscled legs pumping, those broad shoulders slick with sweat, all that wonderful hair flying as he pivoted or leapt. Then there was that look that came into his eyes, wolfish and arrogant.

So, maybe she wanted him to win. That didn't mean she was going to stand up and cheer.

By the third quarter, she was on her feet, like the rest of the crowd, when Ry sank a three-pointer that put the Smoke Eaters over the Bloodhounds by two.

"Nothing but net," she shouted, jostling Cilla. "Did you see that?"

"He's got some great moves," Cilla agreed. "Fast hands."

"Yeah." Natalie felt the foolish grin spread over her face. "Tell me about it."

Heart thumping, she dropped back on the bench. She was leaning forward now, her gaze glued to the ball. The sound of running feet echoed as the men pounded up-court. The cops took a shot, the Smoke Eaters blocked it. The ensuing scuffle left two men on the ground, others snarling in each other's faces as the ref blew his whistle.

Now, Natalie thought grimly, they were playing dirty. With a grunt, she dipped her hand into the bag of salted nuts Cilla offered.

Fast break. Flying elbows, a tangle of bodies under the net as the ball shot up, careened, was pursued.

"Going to put out your fire, Piasecki," one of the cops taunted.

Natalie saw Ry flick the sweaty hair out of his eyes and grin. "Not with that equipment."

Trash talk. Natalie sneered at the cop as she chomped a peanut. No round ball game was complete without it. She hooted down the referee as he stepped between two over-enthusiastic competitors, barely preventing an informal boxing match.

"Boys, boys," Cilla said with a sigh. "They always take their games so seriously."

"Games are serious," Natalie muttered.

It was too close to call. Natalie continued to munch on peanuts as a sensible alternative to her fingernails. When a time-out was called, she glanced at the clock. There was less than six minutes to go, and the Bloodhounds were up, 108 to 105.

On the sidelines, the Smoke Eaters' coach was surrounded by his team. The lanky, silver-haired man was punching his fist into his palm to accentuate whatever instructions he was giving his men. Most were bent at the waist, hands on knees, as they caught their breath for the final battle. As they headed back onto the court, Ry turned. His gaze shot unerringly to Natalie. And he grinned. Quick, cocky, arrogant.

"Wow," Cilla murmured. "Now *that's* serious. Very powerful stuff."

"You're telling me." Natalie blew out a breath. When that did nothing to level her system, she used the excess energy to cheer on her team.

It was a fight to the finish, the lead tipping back to the Smoke Eaters, then sliding away. As time dripped away, second by second, the crowd stayed on its feet, building a wall of sound.

With seconds to go, the Smoke Eaters a point behind, Natalie was chewing on her knuckles. Then she saw Ry make his move. "Oh, yes…" She whispered it first, almost like a prayer. Then she began to shout it as he burst through the line of defense, controlling the ball as if it were attached to the palm of his hand by an invisible string.

They blocked, he pivoted. He had one chance, and he was surrounded. Natalie's heart tripped as he feinted, faked, then sprang off the floor with a turnaround jump shot that found the sweet spot.

The crowd went wild. Natalie knew *she* did, spinning around to hug Allison, then Cilla. What was left of the peanuts flew through the air like rain. The instant the clock ran out, the stands emptied in a surge of bodies onto the court.

She caught a glimpse of Ry a moment before he was swallowed up. She sank back onto the bench with a hand over her heart.

"I'm exhausted." She laughed and rubbed her damp hands on the knees of her jeans. "I've got to sit."

"What a game!" Allison was bouncing up and down in her sneakers. "Wasn't he great? Did you see, Mom? He scored thirty-three points! Wasn't he great?"

"You bet."

"Can we tell him? Can we go down and tell him?"

Cilla studied the jostling crowd, then looked into her daughter's, shining eyes. "Sure. Coming, Natalie?"

"I'll stay here. If you manage to get to him, tell him I'll hang around and wait."

"Okay. You'll bring him to dinner at Deb's tonight?"

Cautious, Natalie drummed her fingers on her knee. "I'll run it by him."

"Bring him," Cilla ordered, then leaned over and kissed Natalie's cheek. "See you later."

Gradually the gym emptied, the fans swarming out to celebrate, the players heading off to shower. Content, Natalie sat in the quiet. It had been her first full day off in six months, and she'd decided it wasn't such a bad way to spend it after all.

And since Ry hadn't actually asked her to come, he was under no real obligation. Neither of them was. Sensibly, neither of them was looking for restrictions, for commitments, for romance. It was simply a primal urge on both parts, fiercely intense now, and very likely to fade.

It was fortunate that they both understood that, right from the beginning. There was some affection between them, naturally. And respect. But this wasn't a relationship, in the true sense of the word. Neither of them wanted that. It was simply an affair—enjoyable while it lasted, no harm done when it ended.

Then he walked out on court, his hair dark and damp from his shower. His gaze swept up and locked on hers.

Oh, boy, was all she could think while her heart turned a long, slow somersault. She was in trouble.

"Good game," she managed, and forced herself to stand and walk down to him.

"It had its moments." He cocked his head. "You know, it's the first time I've seen you dressed in anything but one of those high-class suits."

To cover the sudden rash of nerves, Natalie reached down and picked up one of the game balls. "Jeans and sweaters aren't usually office attire."

"They look good on you, Legs."

"Thanks." She turned the ball in her hand, studying it rather than him. "Allison had the time of her life. It was nice of you to invite her."

"She's a cute kid. They all are. She's got your mouth, you know. And the jawline. She's going to be a real heartbreaker."

"Right now she's more interested in scoring points on court than scoring them with boys." More relaxed, Natalie looked up again, smiling at him. "You scored a few yourself today, Inspector."

"Thirty-three," he said. "But who's counting?"

"Allison." And she had been, too. Carrying the ball, she wandered out on the court. "I take it this was your annual battle against the Bloodhounds."

"Yeah, we take them on once a year. The proceeds go to charity and all that. But mostly we come to beat the hell out of each other."

Head down, she bounced the ball once, caught it. "You never mentioned it. I mean, not until Allison showed up."

"No." He was watching her, intrigued. If he wasn't mistaken, there was a touch of annoyance in her voice. "I guess I didn't."

She turned her head. "Why didn't you?"

Definitely annoyed, he decided, and scratched his cheek. "I didn't figure it would be your kind of thing."

Now her chin angled. "Oh, really?"

"Hey, it's not the opera, or the ballet." He shrugged and tucked his thumbs in his front pockets. "Or a fancy French restaurant."

She let out a slow breath, drew another in. "Are you calling me a snob again?"

Careful, Piasecki, he warned himself. There was definitely a trapdoor here somewhere. "Not exactly. Let's just say I couldn't see someone like you getting worked up over a basketball game."

"Someone like me," she repeated. Stung, she pivoted, planted her feet, and sent the ball sailing toward the hoop. It swished through, bounced on the court. When she looked back at Ry, she had the satisfaction of seeing his mouth hanging open. "Someone like me," she said again, and went to retrieve the ball. "Just what does that mean, Piasecki?"

He got his hands out of his pockets just in time to catch the ball she heaved at him before it thudded into his chest. He passed it back to her, hard, lifting a brow when she caught it.

"Do that again," he demanded.

"All right." Deliberately she stepped behind the three-point line, gauged her shot and let it rip. The whisper of the ball dropping through the hoop made her smile.

"Well, well, well…" This time Ry retrieved the ball himself. He was rapidly reassessing his opponent. "I'm impressed, Legs. Definitely impressed. How about a little one-on-one?"

"Fine." She crouched, circling him as he dribbled.

"You know, I can't—"

Quick as a snake, she darted in, snatched the ball. She executed a perfect lay-up, tapping the ball on the backboard and into the hoop. "I believe that's my point," she said, and passed the ball back to him.

"You're good."

"Oh, I'm better than good." Flicking her hair back, she moved in to block him. "I was all-state in college, pal. Team captain my junior and senior years. Where do you think Allison gets it?"

"Okay, Aunt Nat, let's play ball."

He pivoted away. She was on him like glue. Good moves, he noted. Smooth, aggressive. Maybe he held back. After all, he wasn't about to send a woman to the boards, no matter how much male ego was on the line.

She didn't have the same sensitivity, and turned into his block hard enough to take his breath away.

Frowning, he rubbed the point under his heart where her shoulder had rammed. Her eyes were glittering now, bold as the Emerald City.

"That's a foul."

She stole the ball, made the point with an impressive over-the-shoulder hook. "I don't see a ref."

She had the advantage, and they both knew it. Not only had he played full-out for an entire game, but she'd had that time to assess his technique, study his moves.

And she was better, he had to admit, a hell of a lot better, than half the cops who had gone up against him that afternoon.

And, worse, she knew it.

He scored off her, but it was no easy thing. She was sneaky, he discovered, using speed and grace and old-fashioned guts to make up for the difference in height.

They juggled the lead. She'd shoved the sleeves of her sweater up. She leapt with him, blocking his shot by a fingertip. And, having no compunctions about using whatever talent she had, let her body bump, linger, then slide against his.

His blood heated, as she'd meant it to. Panting, he picked up the ball and stared at her. Her lips were curved smugly, her face was flushed, her hair was tumbled. He realized he could eat her alive.

He moved in quickly, startling her. She let out a squeal when he snatched her around the waist and hauled her over his shoulder. She was laughing when he sent the ball home with his free hand.

"Now that's definitely a foul."

"I don't see any ref." He shifted her, letting gravity take her down until they were face-to-face, her legs clamped at his waist. He reached out, gathered her hair in one hand and pulled her mouth to his.

Whatever breath she had left clogged. Opening to him, she dived into the greedy kiss and demanded more.

The blood drained so quickly, so completely, out of his head, he nearly staggered. With a sudden, voracious appetite, he tore his mouth from hers and devoured the flesh of her throat.

Smooth, salty, with the lingering undertone of that haunting scent she used. His mouth watered.

"There's a storeroom in the back that locks."

Her hands were already tugging at his shirt. Her breathing was ragged. "Then why are we out here?"

"Good question."

With her locked around him, her teeth doing incredible things to his ear, he pushed through the swinging doors and turned into a narrow corridor. Desperate for her, he fumbled at the knob of the storeroom door, swore, then shoved it open. When he slammed it and locked it at their backs, they were closed in a tiny room crammed with sports equipment and smelling of sweat.

Impatient, Natalie tugged at his hair, dragging his mouth back to hers. He nearly tripped over a medicine ball as he looked around frantically for something, anything, that could double as a bed.

He settled on a weight bench with Natalie on his lap.

"I feel like a damn teenager," he muttered, pulling at the snap of her jeans. Beneath the denim, her skin was hot, damp, trembling.

"Me too." Her heart was beating against her ribs like a hammer. "Oh God, I want you. Hurry."

Frantic hands tore at clothes, scattered them. There was no time, no need, for finesse. Only for heat. It was building inside her so fast, so hot, she felt she might implode and there would be nothing left of her but a shell.

His hands were at her throat, her breasts, her hips, thrilling her. Tormenting her. Nothing and no one mattered but him and this wild, incendiary fire they set together.

She wanted it hotter, higher, faster.

With a low, feline sound that shuddered through his blood, she straddled him. His heart seemed to stop in the instant she imprisoned him, as her body arched back, her eyes closing. She filled his vision, his mind, left him helpless. Then her eyes opened again and locked on his.

She began to move, fast and agile. Already it was flash point. He let the power take him, and her.

"I've never done anything like this before." Staggered and spent, Natalie struggled back into her clothes. "I mean *never.*"

"It wasn't exactly the way I'd planned it." Baffled, Ry dragged a hand through his hair.

"We're worse than a couple of kids." Natalie smoothed down her sweater, sighing lavishly. "It was fabulous."

His lips twitched. "Yeah." Then he sobered. "So are you."

She smiled and tried finger-combing her hair into place. "We'd better stop pushing our luck and get out of here. And I've got to get home and change." She discovered that one of her earrings had fallen out, and located it on the floor. "There's dinner at the Guthries' tonight."

He watched her fasten the earring, foolishly charmed by the simple female act. "I'll give you a lift home."

"I'd appreciate it." Feeling awkward, she turned to unlock the door. "You're welcome to come to dinner. I know Boyd wants a chance to talk with you. About the fires."

He closed a hand over hers on the knob. "How's the food?"

She smiled again, looking back at him. "Fabulous."

She was right about the food, Ry discovered. Rack of lamb, fresh asparagus, glossy candied yams, all accompanied by some golden French wine.

He knew, of course, that Gage Guthrie was dripping with money. But nothing had prepared him for the Gothic mansion of a house, with its towers and turrets and terraces. The next thing to a castle, Ry had thought when he viewed it from the outside.

Inside, it was home, rich and elaborate, certainly, but warm. Deborah had given him a partial tour down winding corridors, up curving steps, before they all settled into the enormous dining room with its ox-roasting stone fireplace and winking crystal chandeliers.

It might, Ry thought, have had the flavor of a museum, if not for the people in it.

He'd clicked with Deborah instantly. He'd heard she was a tough and tenacious prosecutor. She had a softer, more vulnerable look than her sister, but she had a reputation for being formidable in court.

It was obvious her husband adored her. There were little signs—the quick, shared looks, the touch of a hand.

It was very much the same between Boyd and Cilla. Ry calculated that they'd been together for a decade or so, but the spark was still very much in evidence.

And the kids were great. He'd always had a soft spot for children. He recognized and was touched by Allison's preadolescent crush, and obliged her by going over the highlights of the game.

Since Cilla had wisely seen to it that her oldest son was across the table and two chairs down from his sister, Bryant was free to badger Deborah about how many bad guys she'd locked up since last he'd seen her.

And dinner was a relatively peaceful affair.

"Do you ride in a fire truck?" Keenan wanted to know.

"I used to," Ry told him.

"How come you stopped?"

"I told you," Bryant said, rolling his eyes with the disdain only a sibling knows and understands. "He goes after bad guys now, like Dad. Only just bad guys who burn things down. Don't you?"

"That's right."

"I'd rather ride in a fire truck." In a canny move to avoid the asparagus on his plate, Keenan slipped out of his chair and into Ry's lap.

"Keenan," Cilla said. "Ry's trying to eat."

"He's okay." Enjoying himself, Ry shifted the boy onto his knee. "Did you ever ride in one?"

"Nuh-uh." He smiled winningly, using his big, soft eyes. "Can I?"

"If your mom and dad say it's okay, you could come down to the station tomorrow. Take a look around."

"Cool." Bryant had immediately picked up on the invitation. "Can we, Dad?"

"I don't see why not."

"Aunt Nat knows where it is," Ry added as Keenan bounced gleefully on his knee. "Make it around ten, and I'll give you a tour."

"Pretty exciting stuff." Cilla rose. "And if we're going to pull it off, I'd say you three better get washed up and bedded down." The knee-jerk protest might have been stronger if not for the long day the children had put in. Cilla merely shook her head, looking at Boyd. "Slick?"

"Okay." He rose and tossed Bryant up and over his shoulder, turning whines into giggles. "Let's move out."

"I'll give you a hand." Natalie plucked Keenan from Ry's lap. "Say good-night, pal."

"Good night, pal," he echoed, and nuzzled into her neck. "You smell as good as Thea, Aunt Nat."

"Thanks, honey."

"Am I going to get a story?"

"Swindler," she laughed and carried him out.

"Nice family," Ry commented.

"We like them." Deborah smiled at him. "You've certainly given them something to look forward to tomorrow."

"No big deal. The guys love to show off for kids. Great meal."

"Frank's one in a million," she agreed. "A former pickpocket." She closed her hand over Gage's. "Who now uses those nimble fingers to create gastronomic miracles. Why don't we have coffee in the small salon? I'll go help Frank with it."

"This is some house," Ry said as he and Gage left the dining room and wound their way toward the salon. "Ever get lost?"

"I've got a good sense of direction."

There was a fire burning in the salon, and the lights were low and welcoming. Again Ry got the impression of home, settled, content.

"You used to be a cop, didn't you?"

Gage stretched out in a chair. "That's right. My partner and I were working on a sting that went wrong. All the way wrong." It still hurt, but the wounds were scarred over now. "He ended up dead, and I was the next thing to it. When I came out of it, I didn't want to pick up a badge again."

"Rough." Ry knew it was a great deal more than that. If he had the story right in his head,

Gage had lingered in a coma for months before facing life again. "So you picked up the family business instead."

"So to speak. We have something in common there. You're running the family business, too."

Ry gave Gage a level look. "So to speak."

"I checked you out. Natalie's important to Deborah, and to me. I can tell you in advance, Boyd's going to ask if she's important to you." He glanced up as Boyd walked in. "That was fast."

"I saw my chance and went over the wall." He dropped into a chair, crossed his feet at the ankles. "So, Piasecki, what's going on between you and my sister?"

Ry decided he'd been polite long enough, and took out a cigarette. He lit it, flipped the match into a spotless crystal ashtray. "I'd say anybody who makes captain on the force should be able to figure that out for himself."

Gage smothered a laugh with a cough as Boyd's eyes narrowed. "Natalie's not a tossaway," Boyd said carefully.

"I know what she is," Ry returned. "And I know what she isn't. If you want to grill someone on what's going on between us, Captain, you'd better start with her."

Boyd considered, nodded. "Fair enough. Give me a rundown on the arson investigation."

That he could, and would, do. Ry related the sequence, the facts, his own steps and conclusions, answering Boyd's terse questions with equal brevity.

"I'm betting on Clarence," he finished. "I know his pattern, and how his warped mind works. And I'll get him," he said, and blew out a last stream of smoke. "That's a promise."

"In the meantime, Natalie needs to beef up security." Boyd's mouth thinned. "I'll see to that."

Ry tapped out his cigarette. "I already have."

"I was talking about personal security, not business."

"So was I. I'm not going to let anything happen to her," he continued as Boyd studied him. "That's another promise."

Boyd let out a snort. "Do you really think she'll listen to you?"

"Yeah. She's not going to get a choice."

Boyd paused, reevaluated. "Maybe I'm going to like you after all, Inspector."

"Okay, break it up," Deborah ordered as she wheeled in a cart laden with a huge silver coffee urn and Meissen china. "I know you're talking shop."

Gage rose to take the cart from her and kiss her. "You're just mad because you might have missed something."

"Exactly."

"Jacoby," Boyd tossed at her. "Clarence Robert. Ring any bells?"

Her brow furrowed as she poured coffee. "Jacoby. Also known as Jack Jacoby?" She served Boyd, took another cup to Ry. "Skipped bail a couple of years ago on an arson charge."

"I like your wife," Ry said to Gage. "There's nothing quite like a sharp mind in a first-class package."

"Thanks." Gage poured a cup for himself. "I often think the same."

"Jacoby," Deborah repeated, focusing on Ry. "You think he's the one?"

"That's right."

"We'd have a file on him." She glanced at her husband. The computers in Gage's hidden room could access everything about Jacoby, right down to his shoe size. "I'm not sure who had the case, but I can find out on Monday, see that you get whatever we have."

"I'd appreciate it."

"How'd he manage bail?" Boyd wanted to know.

"I can't tell you until I see the file," Deborah began.

"I can tell you about him." Ry drank his coffee, keeping one ear out for Natalie's return. He wasn't sure she'd appreciate having her business discussed while she was out of the room. "His pattern's empty buildings, warehouses, condemned apartments. Sometimes the owners hire him for the insurance, sometimes he does it for kicks. We only tried him twice, convicted him once. There wasn't any loss of life either time. Clarence doesn't burn people, just things."

"So now he's loose," Boyd said in disgust.

"For the time being," Ry returned. "We're ready for him." He picked up his cup again when he heard Natalie and Cilla laughing in the hallway.

"You're a softie, Nat."

"It's my duty, and my privilege, to spoil them."

They entered together. Cilla immediately headed for Boyd and dropped into his lap. "They had her jumping through hoops."

"They did not." Natalie poured her coffee, then laughed again. "Not exactly." She smiled at Ry before settling beside him. "So," she began, "have you finished discussing my personal and business life?"

"A sharp mind," Ry commented. "In a first-class package."

Later, as they drove away from the Guthrie mansion, Natalie studied Ry's profile. "Should I apologize for Boyd?"

"He didn't pull out the rubber hoses." Ry shrugged. "He's okay. I've got a couple of sisters, I know how it is."

"Oh." Frowning, she looked out the window. "I didn't realize you had siblings."

"I'm Polish and Irish, and you figured me for an only child?" He grinned at her. "Two older sisters, one in Columbus, the other down in Baltimore. And a brother, a year younger than me, living in Phoenix."

"Four of you," she murmured.

"Until you count the nieces and nephews. There were eight of them, last time I checked, and my brother has another on the way."

Which probably explained why he was so easy around children. "You're the only one who stayed in Urbana."

"Yeah, they all wanted out. I didn't." He turned

down her street, slowed. "Am I staying tonight, Natalie?"

She looked at him again. How could he be so much of a stranger, she wondered, and so much of a need? "I want you to," she said. "I want you."

Chapter 8

"Can I slide down the pole, Mr. Pisessy? Please, can I slide down it?"

Ry grinned at the way Keenan massacred his name and flipped the brim of the boy's baseball cap to the back of his curly head. "Ry."

"'Cause," Keenan said, big eyes sober and hopeful. "I never, ever did it before."

"No, not why, Ry. You call me Ry. And sure you can slide down it. Hold it." Laughing, he caught Keenan at the waist before the boy could make the leap from floor to pole. "No flies on you, huh?"

Keenan looked around, grinned. "Nuh-uh."

"Let's do it this way." With Keenan firmly at his hip, Ry reached out to grip the pole. "Ready?"

"Let's go!"

In a smooth, practiced move, Ry stepped into air. Keenan laughed all the way down.

"Again!" Keenan squealed. "Let's do it again!"

"Your brother wants a turn." Ry looked up, saw Bryant's anxious, eager face in the opening. "Come on, Bryant, go for it."

"Definitely daddy material," Cilla murmured, watching her son zip down the pole.

"Shut up, Cilla." Natalie slipped her hands into the pockets of her blazer. She was itching to try the ride herself.

"Just an observation. Attagirl, Allison," she added, cheering her daughter on when Allison dropped lightly to the floor. "He's giving the kids the time of their lives here."

"I know. It's very sweet of him." She smiled as Ry obliged Keenan with another trip down the pole. "I didn't know he could be sweet."

"Ah, hidden qualities." Cilla glanced over to where Boyd was holding a conversation with two uniformed firefighters. "Often the most attractive kind in a man. Especially when he's crazy about you."

"He's not." It amazed Natalie to feel heat rising to her cheeks. "We're just…enjoying each other."

"Yeah, sure." With a mother's honed reflexes, Cilla crouched and caught her youngest as he flew at her.

"Look, Mom. It's a real, actual fireman's hat." The helmet Ry had given Keenan to wear slipped down over the boy's face. Inside, it smelled mysteriously, fascinatingly, of smoke. "And Ry says we can go sit in the fire engine now." After wriggling down and dancing in place, he shouted at his brother and sister. "Let's go!"

Accompanied by two firefighters, the children dashed off to check out the engine. With a signal to Cilla to wait, Boyd disappeared up the steps with Ry.

"Well." Cilla sniffed and shrugged. "The womenfolk have been dismissed. They'll go upstairs to grunt significantly over official business."

"I wish Boyd wouldn't worry so much. There's really nothing he can do."

"Older siblings are programmed to worry." Cilla slung an arm around Natalie's shoulder. "But, if it helps, he's feeling a lot less worried since he's met Ry."

"That's something, I suppose." Relaxed again, she walked with Cilla toward the back of the engine. "So, how's Althea doing?" Around the front, the children were barraging the firefighters with questions. "The last time I talked to her, she claimed she was as big as two houses and miserably bored with desk duty."

"She's the sexiest expectant mother I've ever seen. Since Colt and Boyd ganged up on her, she's at home on full maternity leave. I dropped over to see her one day a couple of weeks ago and caught her knitting."

"Knitting?" Natalie let out a full-throated laugh. "Althea?"

"Funny what marriage and family can do to you."

"Yeah." Natalie's smile faded a bit. "I suppose that's true."

Upstairs, Boyd was frowning over Ry's reports. "Why upstairs, in the office?" he asked. "Why didn't he start the fire in the showroom? It seems to me there would have been more damage more quickly."

"The showroom window could have put him off. I figure the storeroom would have made more sense if he was just looking to burn the place down. It's private, full of stock and boxes." Ry set aside his coffee. He really had to start cutting down. "I figure he was following instructions. Clarence is real good at following instructions."

"Whose?"

"That's the ticket." Ry kicked back in his chair and propped his feet on his desk. "I've got two incendiary fires that are obviously related. The target in both cases is a single business, and both, I believe, were started by a single perpetrator."

"So he's on somebody's payroll." Boyd set the reports aside. "A competitor?"

"We're checking it out."

"But it's unlikely a competitor would be able to give your pal Clarence access to either building. You didn't find any sign of forced entry."

"That's right." Ry lit a cigarette. A man couldn't cut down on two vices at once. "Which leads us to Natalie's organization."

Boyd got up to pace. "I can't claim to know her staff, certainly not in this new project of hers. I don't deal with the business end of Fletcher unless I'm backed into a corner." He regretted that now, only because he would have been more help if he'd been familiar with her procedures and personnel. "But I can get a lot of information from my parents, particularly on her top people."

"It couldn't hurt. The fact that there was only cosmetic damage at the last fire leads to the conclusion that there'll be another. If Clarence follows his pattern, he'll hit her again within the next ten days." He tossed papers aside. "We'll be waiting for him."

Boyd looked back and measured the man. Tough, smart. But, as he knew from personal experience, the job could get sticky when a man found himself involved with a target.

"And while you're waiting for him, you'll keep Natalie out of it."

"That's the idea."

"And while you're doing that, you're going to be able to separate the woman you're involved with from the case you're trying to close."

Ry lifted a brow. That was going to be a challenge, and the difficulty of meeting that challenge had crossed his mind more than once. The trouble was, he wasn't willing to give up either the woman or the case.

"I know what needs to be done, Captain."

With a nod, Boyd placed his palms on the desk and leaned forward. "I'm trusting you with her,

Piasecki, on every level. If she gets hurt—on any level—I'm coming after you."

"Fair enough."

An hour later, Natalie stood on the curb outside the station, waving goodbye. "You were a big hit, Inspector."

"Hey, a shiny red fire truck, a long brass pole—how could I miss?"

Laughing, she turned to link her arms around his neck. "Thanks." She kissed him lightly.

"For?"

"For being so nice to my family."

"It wasn't a hardship. I like kids."

"It shows. And—" she kissed him again "—that's for putting Boyd's mind at ease."

"I don't know if I'd go quite that far. He's still thinking about punching me out if I make the wrong move with his baby sister."

"Well, then..." Her eyes danced up at his. "You'd better be careful, because my big brother is plenty tough."

"You don't have to draw me a picture." He swung her toward the doors. "Come on back up with me. I need to get a couple of things."

"All right." They'd barely started up the stairs

when the bells sounded. "Oh." The sound of clattering feet echoed below them. "I'm sorry the kids missed this." Then she stopped, wincing. "That's terrible, acting like a fire's a form of entertainment."

"It's a natural reaction. Bells, whistles, men in funny uniforms. It's a hell of a show."

They crossed over to his office. She waited while he sorted through papers. "Do you ever get cats out of trees?"

"Yep. And kid's heads out of the pickets on railings. I got someone's pet iguana out of a sewer pipe once."

"You're joking."

"Hey, we don't joke about rescue."

He looked up and grinned. She looked so tidy, he thought, in her navy blazer and slacks, with the cashmere sweater, red as one of his engines, softly draped at the neck. Her hair was loose, honey gold. When she tucked it behind her ear in that fluid, unconscious movement, he could see the wink of rich blue stones. Sapphires, he assumed. Only the genuine article would suit Natalie Fletcher.

"What is it?" A little self-conscious under his stare, she shifted. "Did Keenan leave something edible smeared on my face?"

"No. You look good, Legs. Want to go somewhere?"

"Go somewhere?" The idea put her off balance. Apart from the challenge of that first meal, they hadn't actually *gone* anywhere.

"Like a movie. Or…" He supposed he could handle it. "A museum or something."

"I… Yes, that'd be nice." It shouldn't be so awkward, she thought, to plan a simple date with someone you'd been sleeping with.

"Which?"

"Either."

"Okay." He stuffed some papers in a battered briefcase. "The guys should have a newspaper downstairs. We'll check it out."

"Fine." When they started out, Natalie glanced first toward the stairs and then back toward the poles. She took a deep breath and gave up. "Ry?"

"Yeah."

"Can I slide down the pole?"

He stopped dead and stared down at her. "You want to slide down the pole?"

Amused at herself, Natalie shrugged her shoulders. "Ry, I've *got* to slide down the pole. It's driving me crazy."

"No kidding?" His grin broke out as he put a

hand on her shoulder and turned her around. "Okay, Aunt Nat. I'll go down first, in case you lose your nerve."

"I'm not going to lose my nerve," she said huffily. "I'll have you know I've been rock-climbing dozens of times."

"There's that height thing again. You get a good grip," he continued, demonstrating. "Swing yourself forward. You can wrap your legs around it as you go down."

He flowed down, smooth and fast. Frowning, she leaned over, peering at him through the opening.

"You didn't wrap your legs around it."

"I don't have to," he said dryly. "I'm a professional. Come on, and don't worry—I'll catch you."

"I don't need you to catch me." Insulted, she tossed back her hair. She reached out, took a good grip on the brass pole, then swung agilely into space.

It took a matter of seconds. Her heart had barely had time to settle before her feet hit the floor. Laughing, she looked longingly up again. "See? I didn't need—" Her boast ended on a squeal of surprise as he scooped her up into his arms. "What?"

"You're a natural." He was grinning as he lowered his mouth to hers. And a constant surprise to him, he thought.

She angled her head, settling her arms comfortably around his neck. "I could do it again."

"If you'd do it in red suspenders, a pair of those really little shorts and let me take a picture, the guys would be very grateful."

She lifted a brow. "I think I'll just make a cash donation to the department."

"It's not the same."

"Inspector?" The dispatcher poked his head out of a doorway. His smile spread slowly at the sight of the woman bundled in Ry's arms. "Suspicious fire over at 12 East Newberry. They want you."

"Tell them I'm on my way." He set Natalie back on her feet. "Sorry."

"It's all right. I know how it is." Her disappointment was completely out of proportion, she lectured herself. "I've got some work I should be catching up on, anyway. I'll grab a cab."

"I'll take you home," Ry told her. "On my way." He steered her toward the bench where she'd left her coat. "Are you just going to be hanging around at the apartment?"

"Yes. There are some spreadsheets I should have looked at yesterday."

"So I'll call you."

As Ry helped her on with her coat, she glanced over her shoulder. "All right."

He turned her completely around and indulged himself with one long, hard kiss. "Tell you what, I'll just come by when I'm done."

Natalie worked on getting her breath back. "Better," she managed. "That's even better."

By the middle of the week, Natalie had discovered that for the first time in memory she was behind on her own personal schedule. Not only had she blown the previous weekend, but she hadn't put in a decent night's work all week.

How could she, when she and Ry were spending every free moment together? Every evening they settled into her apartment, ordered dinner—which more often than not had to be reheated after they'd feasted on each other.

She didn't think of work from the time he arrived on her doorstep until she rushed into her office the next morning.

She didn't think of anything but him.

Besotted was what she was, Natalie admitted as

she stared out her office window. Fascinated by the man, and by what happened every time they got within arm's reach of each other.

It was crazy, of course. She knew it. But it was so wonderful at the moment, it didn't seem to matter.

And she could justify it, since she hadn't yet missed any meetings or business deadlines. Now that Ry had given her the go-ahead, she'd authorized the cleanup and redecorating at the flagship store. The stock there was nearly all in place, and the window-dressing was complete.

It was only a matter of days before the grand opening, nationwide, and there'd been no more incidents. That was how she liked to think of the fires now. As incidents.

She should, of course, be making plans to visit all the branches within the next ten days. But the thought of traveling just then seemed so annoying, so depressing. So lonely.

She could delegate Melvin or Donald to make the tour. It wouldn't even be outside of proper business procedure to do so. But it wasn't her style to delegate what should be done by her.

Maybe, if things got settled somehow, Ry could get a few days off, go with her. It would be wonderful to have company—his company—on a quick business trip. She could put it off until after the grand opening, instead of before, and then—

Turning away from the window, she answered the buzzer on her desk. "Yes, Maureen."

"Ms. Marks to see you, Ms. Fletcher."

"Thanks. Send her in." With an effort, Natalie shifted her personal thoughts to the back of her mind and welcomed her accounting executive. "Deirdre, have a seat."

"I'm sorry I'm so behind." Deirdre blew her choppy bangs out of her eyes before she dropped a thick stack of files on Natalie's desk. "Every time we turn around, the system's down."

Natalie frowned as she picked up the first file. "Have you called in the engineer?"

"He's practically living in my lap." Deirdre plopped into a chair and set one practical flat-heeled shoe on her knee. "He fixes it, we forge ahead, and it goes down again. Believe me, running figures has become a challenge."

"We've still got some time before the end of the quarter. I'll call the computer people myself this afternoon. If their equipment's unstable, they'll have to replace it. Immediately."

"Good luck," Deirdre said dryly. "The good

news is, I was able to run a chart on the early cata-log sales. I think you'll be pleased with the re-sults."

"Mmm, hmm…" Natalie was already flipping through the files. "Fortunately, the fires didn't de-stroy records. You'd have a real accounting night-mare on your hands if it had gotten to the files at the flagship."

"You're telling me." Deirdre rubbed her fin-gers over her eyes. "The way the system's been hiccuping, I'd sweat bullets without those hard copies."

"Well, relax. I've got copies of the copies, as well as the backup disks, tucked away. I was hop-ing to run a full audit by the middle of March." She saw the wince before Deirdre could mask it. "But," she added, leaning back, "if we keep run-ning into these glitches, we'll have to put it off until after the tax-season rush."

"My life for you." Solemnly, Deirdre thumped a fist on her breast. "Now to the nitty-gritty. Your outlay is still within the projected parameters. Barely. With the insurance payments, we'll offset some of that."

Natalie nodded, and made herself focus on bud-gets and percentages.

* * *

A few hours later, in a seedy downtown motel, Clarence Jacoby sat on his sagging bed, lighting matches. His hands were pudgy, smooth as a girl's. Each time he would strike the match and watch the magic flare, waiting, waiting until the heat just kissed the tips of his fingers, before blowing it out.

The ashtray beside him was overflowing with the matches that had already flared and burned. Clarence could entertain himself for hours with nothing more.

He thought nearly every night about burning down the hotel. It would be exciting to start the blaze right in his own room, watch it grow and spread. But he wouldn't be alone, and that stopped him.

Clarence didn't care overmuch about people, or the risk to their lives. He simply preferred to be alone with his fires.

He'd learned not to stay overlong after he'd ignited them. The rippling scars over his neck and chest were daily reminders of how quickly, how fiercely, the dragon could turn, even on one who loved it.

So he contented himself with merely conceiving the fire, basking for a regrettably short time in its heat, before fleeing.

Six months before, in Detroit, he'd torched an abandoned warehouse that the owner had no longer needed or wanted. It was the kind of favor, a profitable one on all sides, that Clarence enjoyed. He had stayed to watch that fire burn. Oh, he'd been out of the building and deep in the shadows. But they'd nearly caught him. Those cops and arson people scanned the crowds at the scene just for a face like his.

A worshipful face. A happy face.

With a giggle, Clarence struck another match. But he'd gotten away. And he'd learned another lesson. It wasn't smart to stay and watch. He didn't need to stay and watch. There were so many fires, so many fierce and beautiful blazes living in his mind and heart, he didn't need to stay.

He had only to close his eyes and see them. Feel them. Smell them.

He was humming to himself when the phone rang. His round, childlike face beamed happily when he heard the sound. Only one person had his number here. And that person would have only one reason to call.

It was time, he knew, to free the dragon again.

* * *

At his desk, Ry pored over lab reports. It was nearly seven, and already dark outside. He'd given up on cutting down on coffee, and drank it hot and black from a chipped mug.

He needed to quit for the day. He recognized the slow process of shutting down in his mind and body. Somehow or other, in the past couple of weeks, he'd gotten into a routine he was now beginning to depend on.

No, not somehow or other, Ry reminded himself, scrubbing his hands over his face. Someone.

He was getting much too used to knocking off for the day and heading for her apartment. He even had a key to her front door in his pocket now. Something that had been given and taken without ceremony. As if neither of them wanted to acknowledge what that simple piece of metal stood for.

They'd have a meal, he thought. They'd talk, maybe watch one of the old movies on television—something they'd discovered by accident they both loved.

Most of what they'd discovered about each other, he mused, had been by accident. Or by observation.

He knew she liked long bubble baths in the evening, with the water too hot and a glass of chilled wine sitting on the rim of the tub. She stepped out of those ankle-breakers she wore the minute she walked in the door. And she put everything away in its place.

She slept in silk and hogged the blankets. Her alarm went off at seven on the dot every morning, and if he wasn't quick enough to delay her, she was out of the bed seconds later.

She had a weakness for strawberry ice cream and big-band music.

She was loyal and smart and strong.

And he was in love with her.

Sitting back, Ry rested his eyes. A problem, he thought. His problem. They'd had an unspoken agreement going in, and he knew it. No ties, no tangles.

He didn't want them.

God knew he couldn't afford them with her.

They were opposites on every level but one. The physical needs that had brought them together, no matter how intense, couldn't override everything else. Not in the long term.

So there couldn't be a long term.

He would do what was smart, what was right,

and see her through the arson investigation. And that would be that. Would have to be that.

And to save them both an unpleasant scene, he'd start backing away a little. Starting now.

He rose and grabbed his jacket. He wouldn't go to her place tonight. He looked guiltily at the phone, thinking of calling her, making some excuse.

With an oath, he turned out the lights. He wasn't her damn husband, he reminded himself.

He never would be.

Compelled by a nagging sense of unrest, like an itch between his shoulder blades, Ry drove out to Natalie's plant. He'd done a great deal of driving around since he left the station.

It was after ten o'clock now, moonless, windless.

He sat in his car, slumped behind the wheel, and tried not to think of her.

Of course, he thought of her.

She was probably wondering where he was, he figured. She'd assume he'd gotten a call. She'd wait up. Guilt worked at him again. It was his least favorite emotion. It wasn't right to be inconsiderate, to worry her just because he'd had a scare.

And maybe he wasn't in love with her. Maybe he was just hung up. A man could get hung up on a woman without wanting to slit his throat when she walked away. Couldn't he?

Disgusted, Ry reached for his car phone. The least he could do was call and tell her he was busy. It wasn't like checking in, he assured himself. It was just being polite.

And since when had he worried about manners?

Cursing, he began to dial.

But the itch came back. Slowly, his eyes scanning the dark, he replaced the phone. Had he heard something? A check of his watch told him the patrol he'd assigned would make their run by in another ten minutes.

No harm, he decided, in taking a look around himself on foot in the meantime.

He eased his door open and slipped out. He could hear nothing now but the faint swish of traffic two blocks away. Cautious, he reached back in the car for his flashlight, but he didn't turn it on.

Not yet, he thought. His eyes were accustomed enough to the dark for him to see where he was going.

Instinct had him heading silently around the back.

He'd already cased the plant himself, noting where the exits were located, the security, the fire doors. He'd make a circle, check each door and window on the main level himself.

He heard it again, the scrape of a foot over gravel. Ry shifted the flashlight in his hand, holding it like a weapon now as he moved closer. Tensed, ready, he slipped through the shadows. If it was the security guard, Ry knew, he was about to give the man the fright of his life. Otherwise…

A giggle. Faint and delighted. The slow, moaning whine of a metal door moving on its hinges.

Ry flashed on his light, and spotlighted Clarence Jacoby.

"How's it going, Clarence?" Ry grinned as the man blinked against the glare. "I've been waiting for you."

"Who's that?" Clarence's voice raced up a register. "Who's that?"

"Hey, I'm hurt." Ry lowered the light out of Clarence's eyes and stepped closer. "Don't you recognize your old pal?"

Squinting, Clarence separated the man from the shadows. In a moment, his baffled face exploded in a wide grin. "Piasecki. Hey, Ry

Piasecki. How's it going? You're Inspector now, right? I hear you're an inspector now."

"That's right. I've been looking for you, Clarence."

"Oh, yeah?" Shyly Clarence dipped his head. "How come?"

"I put out that little campfire you started the other night. You must be losing your touch, Clarence."

"Oh, hey…" Still grinning, Clarence spread his arms out. "I don't know nothing about that. You remember when we got burned, Piasecki? Hell of a night, wasn't it? That dragon was really big. Almost ate us up."

"I remember."

Clarence moistened his lips. "Scared you bad, too. I heard the nurses talking in the burn ward about the nightmares."

"I had a few of them."

"And you don't fight fire no more, do you? Don't want to slay the dragon now, do you?"

"I like squashing little bugs like you better." Ry swung his light down, shone it on the gas cans at Clarence's feet. "What do you know, Clarence? You still use premium grade, too."

"I didn't do nothing." Clarence whirled to make

a dash into the dark. Even as Ry leapt forward, the man jerked back, as if on a string.

Staggered, Ry stared at the dark-clad arms that seemed to shoot straight out from the building's wall and wrap around Clarence's neck.

Then it was a shadow flowing out of nothing. Then it was a man flowing out of the shadow.

"I don't believe the inspector was finished talking to you, Clarence." Nemesis kept one arm hooked around Clarence's neck as he faced Ry. "Were you, Inspector?"

"No, I wasn't." Ry let out a long breath. "Thanks."

"My pleasure."

"It's a ghost. A ghost's got me." Clarence's eyes turned up, white, and he fainted dead away.

"I imagine you could have handled him on your own." Nemesis passed the limp body to Ry, waiting until Ry had hefted Clarence over his shoulder.

"I appreciate it, anyway."

There was a quick flash of teeth as Nemesis smiled. "I like your style, Inspector."

"Same goes. You want to explain that little trick when you came out of the wall?" Ry began, but he was talking to air before the sentence was finished.

"Not bad," he muttered, and was shaking his head as he carted Clarence to the car. "Not bad at all."

The phone awakened Natalie from where she'd dozed off on the couch. Groggy, she stumbled toward it, trying to read the time on her watch.

"Yes, hello?"

"It's Ry."

"Oh." She rubbed the sleep from her eyes. "It's after one. I was—"

"Sorry to wake you."

"No, it's not that. I just—"

"We've got him."

"What?" Her irritation that he had yet to let her finish a sentence sharpened the word.

"Clarence. I picked him up tonight. I thought you'd want to know."

Now her head was reeling. "Yes, of course. That's wonderful. But when—?"

"I'm tied up here, Natalie. I'll get back to you when I can."

"All right, but—" She took the receiver away from her ear and glared at the dial tone. "Congratulations, Inspector," she muttered, and hung up.

With her hands on her hips, she took several deep breaths to calm herself, and to clear her head.

She'd been worried sick. Her own fault, she admitted. Ry was certainly under no obligation to come to her after work, or to call. Even if he had been doing just that for days. And even if she had waited by the phone for hours until simple fatigue spared her the continued humiliation.

Put that aside, she ordered herself. The important matter here was that Clarence Jacoby was in custody. There would be no more fires—no more incidents.

And in the morning, she promised herself as she stomped bad-temperedly off to the bedroom, she'd track Ry down and get the whole story.

In the meantime, she thought as she slipped out of her robe, all she had to do was teach herself to sleep alone again.

Even as she settled onto the pillow, she knew it was going to be a very long night.

Chapter 9

Since there seemed little point in going home after he'd finished at the police station, Ry dropped down on the sagging sofa in his office and caught three hours' sleep before the sirens awakened him.

Following old habit, his feet hit the floor before he remembered he didn't have to answer the bell any longer. Years of training would have allowed him to simply roll over and go back to sleep. Instead, he staggered, bleary-eyed, toward the coffeepot, measuring, flipping switches. His only goal at the moment was to take a giant mug of coffee to the showers with him, and to stay there for an hour.

He lit a cigarette, scowling at the pot as it filled, drop by stingy drop.

The brisk knock on his door only made his scowl deepen. Turning, he aimed his bad temper at Natalie.

"Your secretary isn't in."

"Too early," he mumbled, and rubbed a hand over his face. Why in hell did she always have to look so perfect? "Go away, Natalie. I'm not awake yet."

"I won't go away." Struggling not to be hurt, she set her briefcase down, put her hands on her hips. Obviously, she told herself, he'd had little or no sleep. She'd be patient. "Ry, I need to know what happened last night, so I can plan what steps need to be taken."

"I told you what happened."

"You weren't very generous with details."

Muttering, he snatched up a mug and poured the miserly half cup that had brewed. "We got your torch. He's in custody. He won't be lighting any fires for a while."

Patience, Natalie reminded herself and took a seat. "Clarence Jacoby?"

"Yeah." He looked at her. What choice did he have? She was there, stunning and polished and perfect. "Why don't you go to work, let me pull it together here? I'll have a report for you."

Nerves jittered up her spine, and down again. "Is something wrong?"

"I'm tired," he snapped. "I can't get a decent cup of coffee, and I need a shower. And I want you to stop breathing down my neck."

Surprise registered first, then retreated behind hurt. "I'm sorry," she said, voice cool and stiff, as she rose. "I was concerned about what happened last night. And I wanted to make sure you were all right. Since I can see that you are fine…" She picked up her briefcase. "And since you haven't had time to put your report together, I'll get out of your way."

He swore, dragging a hand through his hair. "Natalie, sit down. Please," he added, when she just stood aloofly in the doorway. "I'm sorry. I'm feeling a little raw this morning, and you made the mistake of being the first person in the line of fire."

"I was worried about you." She said it quietly, but didn't step back into the room.

"I'm fine." Turning away, he topped off his coffee. "Want some of this?"

"No. I should have waited for you to contact me. I realize that." It was, she thought, like suddenly walking on eggshells. One night apart shouldn't make them so awkward with each other.

"If you had, I'd have been worried about you." He managed a smile. It was low, he decided, real low, to lash out at her because all at once he was deathly afraid of where they were heading. "Sit down. I'll give you the highlights."

"All right."

While she did, he walked around his desk and kicked back in his chair. "I had an itch, a hunch. Whatever. I decided to take a run by your plant— take a look around, check the security myself." He blew out a stream of smoke, smiled through it. "Somebody else had the same idea."

"Clarence."

"Yeah, he was there. It was a real party. He'd knocked out the alarm. Had himself a full set of keys to the rear door."

"Keys." Eyes sharpening, Natalie leaned forward.

"That's right. Shiny new copies. The cops have them now. There wouldn't have been any sign of break-in. He also had a couple of gallons of high-test gas, a few dozen matchbooks. So we started to have a little conversation. I guess Clarence didn't like the way it was going, and he made a break for it."

Ry paused, drawing in smoke, shaking his head. "I've never seen anything like it," he murmured. "I'm still not sure I *did* see it."

"What?" Impatient, Natalie rapped a hand on his desk. "Did you chase him?"

"Didn't have to. Your pal took care of it."

"My pal?" Baffled she sat back again. "What pal?"

"Nemesis."

Her eyes went wide and stunned. "You saw him? He was there?"

"Yes and no. Or no and yes. I'm not sure which. He came out of the wall," Ry said, half to himself. "He came out of the damn wall, like smoke. He wasn't there, then he was. Then he wasn't."

Natalie cocked a brow. "Ry, I really think you need some sleep."

"No question about that." Rubbing the back of his stiff neck, he blew out a breath. "But that's how it went. He came out of the wall. First his arms. I was standing a foot away, and I saw arms come out of the wall and grab Clarence. Then he was just there—Nemesis. Clarence took one look at him and fainted." Enjoying the memory, Ry grinned. "Folded up like a deck chair. So Nemesis hands him over to me and I haul him over my shoulder. Then he's gone."

"Clarence?"

"Nemesis. Keep up."

She blinked, trying to. "He—Nemesis—just left?"

"He just went. Back into the wall, into the air." He flicked his fingers to demonstrate. "I don't know. I probably stood there for five minutes with my mouth hanging open before I carried Clarence to the truck."

Brow knit, Natalie spoke slowly, carefully. "You're telling me the man disappeared. In front of your eyes. Just vanished?"

"That's exactly what I'm telling you."

"Ry," she said, still patient. "That's not possible."

"I was there," he reminded her. "You weren't. Clarence came to and started babbling about ghosts. He was so spooked he tried to jump out of the car while I was driving." Ry sipped at his coffee. "I had to knock him out."

"You...you knocked him out."

It was another memory he couldn't help but

relish. One short punch to that moon-shaped jaw. "He was better off. Anyway, he's in custody now. He's not talking, but I'm going to interview him in a couple hours and see if we can change that."

She sat silently for a moment, trying to absorb it all, and sort it out. The business with Nemesis was fascinating, and not so difficult to explain. It had been dark. Ry was a trained observer, but even he could make a mistake in the dark. People didn't just vanish.

Rather than argue with him about it, she focused on Clarence Jacoby. "He hasn't said why, then? If he was hired, or by whom?"

"Right now he's claiming he was just out for a walk."

"With several gallons of gasoline?"

"Oh, he says I must have brought the gas with me. I'm framing him because I got burned saving his worthless life."

Insulted, Natalie lunged to her feet. "No one believes that."

Her instant defense amused and touched him. "No, Legs, nobody's buying it. We've got him cold on this one, and it shouldn't take long for the cops to tie him in with the other fires. Once Clarence realizes he's looking at a long stretch, he's likely to sing a different tune. Nobody likes to go down alone."

Natalie nodded. She didn't believe in honor among thieves. "If and when he does name someone, I'll need to know right away. I'm limited as to the steps I can take in the meantime."

Ry rapped his fingers on the desk. He didn't like the possibility that someone in her organization, someone who might be close to her, could be behind the fires. "If Clarence points the finger at one of your people, the cops take the steps. And they're going to be a lot tougher on them than just firing them or taking away their dental plan."

"I'm aware of that. I'm also aware that even though the man who held the match has been caught and my property is safe, it's not over." But the tension that had knotted her shoulders was smoothing away. "I appreciate you looking out for what's mine, Inspector."

"That's what your tax dollars are for." He studied her over the rim of his cup. "I missed being with you last night," he said, before he could stop himself.

Her lips curved slowly. "Good. Because I missed being with you. We could make up for it tonight. Celebrate seeing my tax dollars at work."

"Yeah." If he was sinking, Ry thought, he just didn't have the energy to fight going under for the third time. "Why don't we do that?"

"I'll let you get that shower." She bent down for her briefcase. "Will you let me know what happens when you talk to Clarence?"

"Sure. I'll be in touch."

"I'm going to plan on getting home early," she said as she headed for the door.

"Good plan," he murmured when the door shut behind her. Third time, hell, he thought. He'd drowned days ago, and hadn't even noticed.

Natalie arrived at work with a spring in her step, and called a staff meeting. By ten she was seated at the head of the table in the boardroom, her department heads lining both sides of the polished mahogany.

"I'm pleased to announce that the national grand opening of Lady's Choice will remain, as scheduled, for this coming Saturday."

As expected, there were polite applause and congratulatory murmurs.

"I'd like to take this opportunity," she continued, "to thank you all for your hard work and dedication. Launching a new company of this size

takes teamwork, long hours, and constant innova-
tion. I'm grateful to all of you for giving me your
best. I particularly appreciate all of your help in
the past couple of weeks, when the company faced
such unexpected difficulties."

She waited until the murmurs about the fires
had died down.

"I'm aware that our budget is stretched, but I'm
also aware that we wouldn't be on schedule without the extra effort each one of you, and your staff,
have given. Therefore, Lady's Choice is pleased
to present bonuses to each and every employee on
the first of next month."

This announcement was greeted with a great
deal of enthusiasm. Only Deirdre winced and
rolled her eyes. Natalie flashed a grin at her that
held more pleasure than apology.

"We still have a great deal of work ahead of us,"
Natalie went on. "I'm sure Deirdre will tell you that
I've given her an enormous headache, rather than
a bonus." Natalie waited for the laughter to subside.
"I have faith in her, and in Lady's Choice warrant-
ing it. In addition…" She paused, the smile still in
place, her gaze sweeping from face to face. "I want
to ease everyone's mind. Last night the arsonist
was apprehended. He's now in police custody."

There was applause, a barrage of questions. Natalie sat with her hands folded on the table, watching for, waiting for, some sign that would tell her if one of the people sitting with her had begun to sweat.

"I don't have all the details," she said, holding up a hand for quiet. "Only that Inspector Piasecki apprehended the man outside our plant. I expect a full report within forty-eight hours. In the meantime, we can all thank the diligence of the fire and police departments, and get on with our jobs."

"Was there a fire at the plant?" Donald wanted to know. "Was anything damaged?"

"No. I do know that the suspect was caught before he entered the building."

"Are they sure it's the same one who started the fires at the warehouse and the flagship?" Brow furrowed, Melvin tugged at his bow tie.

Natalie smiled. "As a sister of a police captain, I'm certain the authorities won't make a statement like that until they have absolute proof. But that's the way it looks."

"Who is he?" Donald demanded. "Why did he do it?"

"Again, I don't have all the details. He's a known arsonist. A professional, I believe. I'm sure the motive will come to light before too long."

* * *

Ry wasn't nearly as certain. By noon, he'd been with Jacoby for an hour, covering the same ground. The interrogation room was typically dull. Beige walls, beige linoleum, the wide mirror that everyone knew was two-way glass. He sat on a rock-hard chair, leaning against the single table, smoking lazily, while Clarence grinned and toyed with his own fingers.

"You know they're going to lock the door on you, Clarence," Ry said. "By the time you get out this round, you'll be so old, you won't be able to light a match by yourself."

Clarence grinned and shrugged his shoulders. "I didn't hurt nobody. I never hurt nobody." He looked up then, his small, pale eyes friendly. "You know, some people like to burn other people. You know that, don't you, Ry?"

"Yeah, Clarence, I know that."

"Not me, Ry. I never burned nobody." The eyes lit up happily. "Just you. But that was an accident. You got scars?"

"Yeah, I got scars."

"Me too." Clarence giggled, pleased that they shared something. "Wanna see?"

"Maybe later. I remember when we got burned, Clarence."

"Sure. Sure you do. Like a dragon's kiss, right?"

Like being in the bowels of hell, Ry thought. "The landlord paid you to light the dragon that time, remember?"

"I remember. Nobody lived there. It was just an old building. I like old, empty buildings. The fire just eats along, sniffs up the walls, hides in the ceiling. It talks to you. You've heard it talk, haven't you?"

"Yeah, I've heard it. Who paid you this time, Clarence?"

Playfully Clarence put the tips of his fingers together, making a bridge. "I never said anybody paid me. I never said I did anything. You could've brought the gas, Ry. You're mad at me for burning you." Suddenly his smile was crafty. "You had nightmares in the burn ward. I heard about them. Nightmares about the dragon. And now you don't slay the dragon anymore."

The throb behind his eyes had Ry reaching for another cigarette. Clarence was fascinated by the nightmares, had probed time and again during the interview for details. Even if he'd wanted to, Ry couldn't have given many. It was all a blur of fire and smoke, blessedly misted with time.

"I had nightmares for a while. I got over it. I got

over being mad at you, too, Clarence. We were both just doing our job, right?"

Ry caught the glint in Clarence's eyes when the match was lit. Experimentally, Ry held the small flame between them. "It's powerful, isn't it?" he murmured. "Just a little flame. But you and me, we know what it can do—to wood, paper. Flesh. It's powerful. And when you feed it, it gets stronger and stronger."

He touched the match to the tip of his cigarette. Still watching Clarence, Ry licked his forefinger and snuffed out the flame. "Douse it with water, cut off its air, and *poof.*" He tossed the broken match into the overburdened ashtray. "We both like to control it, right?"

"Yeah." Clarence licked his lips, hoping Ry would light another match.

"You get paid for starting them. I get paid for putting them out. Who paid you, Clarence?"

"They're going to send me up anyway."

"Yeah. So what have you got to lose?"

"Nothing." Sly again, Clarence looked up at Ry through thin, pale lashes. "I'm not saying I started any fire. But if we was to suppose *maybe* I did, I couldn't say who asked me to."

"Why not?"

"Because if we was to suppose I did, I never saw who asked me to."

"Did you talk to him?"

Clarence began to play with his fingers again, his face so cheerful Ry had to grit his teeth to keep himself from reaching out and squeezing the pudgy neck. "Maybe I talked to somebody. Maybe I didn't. But maybe if I did, the voice on the phone was all screwed up, like a machine."

"Man or woman?"

"Like a machine," Clarence repeated, gesturing toward Ry's tape recorder. "Maybe it could have been either. Maybe they just sent me money to a post-office box before, and after."

"How'd they find you?"

Clarence moved his right shoulder, then his left. "Maybe I didn't ask. People find me when they want me." His grin lit his face. "Somebody always wants me."

"Why that warehouse?"

"I didn't say nothing about a warehouse," Clarence said, pokering up.

"Why that warehouse?" Ry repeated. "Maybe."

Pleased that Ry was playing the game, Clarence scooted forward in his chair. "Maybe for the insurance. Maybe because somebody didn't like who owned the place. Maybe for fun. There's lots of reasons for fire."

Ry pressed him. "And the store. The same person owned the store."

"There were pretty things in the store. Pretty girl things." Forgetting himself, Clarence smiled in reminiscence. "It smelled pretty, too. Even prettier after I poured the gas."

"Who told you to pour the gas, Clarence?"

"I didn't say I did."

"You just did."

Clarence pouted like a child. "Did not. I said maybe."

The tape would prove different, but Ry kept his probing steady. "You liked the girl things in the store."

Clarence's eyes twinkled. "What store?"

Biting back an oath, Ry leaned back. "Maybe I should call my friend back and let him talk to you."

"What friend?"

"From last night. You remember last night."

All color drained from Clarence's face. "He was a ghost. He wasn't really there."

"Sure he was there. You saw him. You felt him."

"A ghost." Clarence began to gnaw on his fingernails. "I didn't like him."

"Then you'd better talk to me, or I'm going to have to go get him."

Panicked, Clarence darted his eyes around the room. "He's not here."

"Maybe he is," Ry said, enjoying himself. "Maybe he isn't. Who paid you, Clarence?"

"I don't know." His lips began to tremble. "Just a voice. That's all. Take the money and burn. I like money, I like to burn. Started on the nice shiny desk in the store with the girl things, just like the voice said to. Coulda done better in the storeroom, but the voice said do the desk." Uneasy, he looked around. "Is he in here?"

"What about the envelopes? Where are the envelopes the money came in?"

"Burned them." Clarence grinned again. "I like to burn things."

Natalie very nearly burned the chicken.

It wasn't that she was incompetent in the kitchen. It was simply, she told herself, that she rarely found the opportunity to use the culinary skills she possessed—meager though they might be.

With a great deal of cursing and trepidation, she removed the browned chicken from the skillet and set it aside, as per Frank's meticulous directions.

By the time she had the sauce simmering, she was feeling smug. Cooking wasn't really such a big deal, she decided, if you just concentrated and went step-by-step. Read the recipe as if it were a contract, she thought, carefully sliding the chicken into the sauce. Overlook no clause, study the small print. And... Humming to herself, she set the cover on the skillet, then looked around at the wreck of her kitchen.

And, she decided, blowing the hair out of her eyes, clean up after yourself—because no deal should ever look as though you'd sweat over it.

It took her longer to set the kitchen, and herself, to rights than it had to prepare the meal. After one quick glance at the time, she dashed to light the candles and create the mood.

With a long sigh, she dropped onto the arm of the sofa and scanned the room. Soft lights, quiet music, the scent of flowers and good food, the golden glow of sedate flames in the hearth. Pleased, Natalie smoothed a hand down her long silk skirt. Everything was perfect, she decided.

Now where was Ry?

He was pacing the hallway outside her door.

Making too big a deal out of it, Piasecki, he warned himself. You're just two people enjoying each other. No strings, no promises. Now that Clarence was in custody, they would start to drift apart. Naturally. No sweat, no strain.

So why in the hell was he standing outside her door, nervous as a teenager on a first date? Why was he holding a bunch of stupid daffodils in his hand?

He should never have brought her flowers in the first place, he decided. But if he'd had the urge, he should have gone for roses, at least, or orchids. Something with class. Just because the yellow blooms had caught his eye and the street vendor had been pushing them, that was no reason to dump a bunch of backyard flowers on a woman like Natalie.

He thought seriously about dropping them in front of her neighbor's door. The idea made him feel even more foolish. Muttering under his breath, he pulled out his key and unlocked the door.

Coming home. It was a ridiculous sensation, walking into an apartment that wasn't his. But it was there, as bold as a ten-foot sign, as subtle as a peck on the cheek.

She rose from her perch on the couch and smiled at him. "Hi."

"Hi."

He had the flowers behind his back, hardly realizing the move was defensive. She looked incredible, the thin-strapped, flowing dress—the color of ripe peaches—skimming down, candle and firelight flickering over her. When she moved, he swallowed. The dress sliced open from the ankle to the trio of gold buttons running down her left hip.

"Long day," she asked, and kissed him lightly on the mouth.

"Yeah. I guess." His tongue had tied itself into knots. "You?"

"Not too bad. The good news has everybody pumped up. I have some wine chilling." She tilted her head, smiling at him. "Unless you'd rather have a beer."

"Whatever," he murmured as she strolled toward the table by the window, which she had set for two. "It looks nice in here. You look nice."

"Well, I thought, since we were celebrating…" She poured two glasses. "I had planned on doing this after the grand opening on Saturday, but it seems appropriate now." With the glasses on the table behind her, she held out a hand. "I have a lot to thank you for."

"No, you don't. I did what I was paid to do…." He trailed off, seeing that her gaze had shifted, softened. With some discomfort, he realized it was riveted on the flowers he'd used to gesture her thanks away.

"You brought me flowers." The simple shock in her voice didn't help his nerves.

"This guy on the corner was selling them, and I just—"

"Daffodils," she said with a sigh. "I love daffodils."

"Yeah?" Miserably awkward, he thrust them at her. "Well, here you go."

Natalie buried her face in the bright trumpets and, for reasons she couldn't fathom, wanted to weep. "They're so pretty, so happy." She lifted her head again, eyes glowing. "So perfect. Thank you."

"It's no big—" But the rest of his words were cut off when her mouth closed over his.

Instant desire. Like a switch flicked on inside him. One touch, he thought as his arms came hard around her, and he wanted her. Her body molded to his, her arms circled. He fought back a desperate need to drag her to the floor and release the helpless passion she stirred up inside him.

"You're tense," she murmured, stroking a hand over his shoulders. "Did something happen with Clarence during the interview that you didn't tell me?"

"No." Clarence Jacoby and his moon-pie face were the last things on Ry's mind. "I'm just wired, I guess." And in need of some basic control. "Something smells good," he said as he eased back. "Besides you."

"Frank's fricassee."

"Frank's?" Taking another step back, Ry reached for his wine. "Guthrie's cook made us dinner?"

"No, it's his recipe." She tucked her hair behind her ear. "I made us dinner."

Ry snorted into his wine. "Yeah. Right. Where'd you get it? The Italian place?"

Torn between amusement and insult, Natalie took her wine. "*I* made it, Piasecki. I know how to turn on a stove."

"You know how to pick up the phone and order." More relaxed now, Ry took her hand and pulled her toward the kitchen. He walked directly to the skillet and lifted the lid. It certainly looked homemade. Frowning, he sniffed at the thick, bubbling sauce covering the golden pieces of chicken. "You cooked this? Yourself?"

Exasperated, Natalie tugged her hand away and sipped her wine. "I don't see why that should be such a shock. It's just a matter of following directions."

"You cooked this," he said again, shaking his head. "How come?"

"Well, because… I don't know." With a little snap of metal on metal, she covered the skillet again. "I felt like it."

"I just can't picture you puttering around the kitchen."

"There wasn't a lot of puttering." Then she laughed. "And it wasn't a very pretty sight. So, no matter what it tastes like, you're required to praise, lavishly. I need to put the flowers in water."

He waited while she got a vase and arranged the daffodils on the kitchen counter.

She looked softer tonight, he thought. All feminine and cozy. And she handled each individual bloom as though he'd brought her rubies. Unable to resist, he lifted his hand to stroke it gently down her hair. She looked up, with surprise, her uncertainty at the show of tenderness evident.

"Is something wrong?"

"No." Cursing himself, he dropped his hand to his side. "I like to touch you."

Her eyes cleared, danced. "I know." She turned into his arms, inviting. "The chicken needs to simmer for a while." She nipped lightly, teasingly, at his lip. "An hour, anyway. Why don't we—"

"Sit down," he finished, to keep from exploding. He was not, he absolutely was not, going to drag her down and take her on the kitchen floor.

"Okay." Left uneasy by his withdrawal, she nodded and picked up her wine again. "We should enjoy the fire."

In the living room, she curled up next to him and rested her head on his shoulder. Obviously, he had something on his mind. She could wait for him to share it with her. It was lovely just sitting here, she thought with a sigh, watching the fire together as dinner cooked and an old Cole Porter tune drifted through the speakers.

It was as if they sat like this every night. Comfortable with each other, knowing there was time, all the time in the world simply to be. After a long, busy day, what better end could there be than to sit beside someone you loved and—

Oh, God. Her thoughts had her jerking straight upright. *Loved.* She loved him.

"What's wrong?"

"Nothing." She swallowed hard, fought to keep her voice even. "Just something I…forgot. I can deal with it later."

"No shoptalk, okay?"

"No." She took a hasty sip of wine. "Fine."

She couldn't get a decent night's sleep when he wasn't beside her. She'd had an irresistible urge to cook him a meal. Her heart turned over every time he smiled at her. She'd even been rerouting a business trip with him in mind.

Oh, why hadn't she seen it before? It had been staring her in the face every time she looked in the mirror.

What was she going to do?

Closing her eyes, she ordered her body to relax. Her emotions were her problem, she reminded herself. She was a grown woman who had gone into an affair with the rules plain on both sides. She couldn't—wouldn't—change the terms in midstream.

What was needed was some clear and careful thought. Some time, she added, concentrating on breathing evenly. Then a plan. She was an excellent planner, after all.

His fingertips brushed lightly over her shoulder. Her pulse scrambled.

"I'd better check on dinner."

"It hasn't been an hour." He liked the way she was curled against him, and wanted to keep her there. Stupid to be worried about where they were heading, he decided, letting himself get drunk on the smell of her hair. Where they were now was exactly the right place to be.

"I was…going to make a salad," she said uncertainly.

"Later."

He slid his fingers under her chin and turned her face toward his. Odd, he thought, it seemed as though his nerves had drained out of him and into her. Experimentally he dipped his head, letting his lips cruise over hers.

She trembled against him.

Intrigued, he drew her lower lip into his mouth, bathing it with his tongue while his eyes watched emotions come and go in hers.

She shuddered.

"Why are we always in a hurry?" he murmured, addressing the question as much to himself as to her.

"I don't know." She had to get away, clear her head, before she made some foolish mistake. "We need more wine."

"I don't think so." Slowly he brushed the hair back from her face so that he could frame it with his hands. He held her there, his eyes on hers. "Do you know what I think, Natalie?"

"No." She moistened her lips, struggling to find her balance.

"I think we've missed a step here."

"I don't know what you mean."

He pressed his lips to her brow, drew back, and watched her eyes cloud. "Seduction," he whispered.

Chapter 10

Seduction? She didn't need to be seduced. She wanted him, always wanted him. Before she realized she loved him, she had equated her response to him as a kind of volatile chemical reaction. But now, couldn't he see…

Her thoughts trailed off into smoke as his lips roamed lazily down her temple.

"Ry." She put her hand to his chest, told herself she would keep her voice light, joking…disentangle herself long enough to clear her mind and regain her balance. But his fingers were stroking along her collarbone, and his mouth was nipping closer, closer to hers. She only said, "Ry," again.

"We're good at moving straight ahead, you and me, aren't we, Natalie?" But now there was something smooth and easy gliding through him. Fascinated by his own reaction, he traced his tongue over her lips. "Fast, with no detours, that's us. I think it's time we took a little side trip."

"I think…" But she couldn't think. Not after his mouth fit itself to hers. He'd never kissed her like this before, never like this, so slow, so deep, with a lazy kind of possession that shot simmering heat straight to the marrow of her bones.

Her body went lax, as fluid as the wax pooling the wicks of the candles around them. Beneath her palm, his heart beat hard, and not quite steady, and the low, helpless sound that vibrated in her throat quickened it. Yet he continued that slow, deep exploration of her mouth, as if he would be content with that, only that, for hours.

Her head fell back. He cupped it, shifting her slightly to change the angle of the kiss, toying with her lips, her tongue. Her breath caught and released, caught and released, shuddering once when his fingers brushed up over her breast.

Now, she knew, now would come the speed and the power she understood. There would be control again, in the sheer lack of control as they rushed to take each other. But his fingers simply skimmed up her throat and lay with devastating tenderness on her cheek.

In defense, she reached for him, pulling him tight against her.

"Not this time." He drew back just enough to study her face. Confusion, need, and arousal made a beautiful combination. However much his own blood was pounding, he intended to confuse her more, intended to see to each and every need, and arouse her until her body was limp.

"I want you." She tore hurriedly at the buttons of his shirt. "Now, Ry. I want you now."

He pulled her down on the floor in front of the fire. The light from the flames flickered over her skin, danced in her hair. She was golden. Like some exotic treasure a man might spend his life in search of. And for now, for tonight, Ry thought, she was only his.

He stretched her arms out to the sides, linked his fingers with hers. "You'll have to wait," he told her. "Until I'm finished seducing you."

"I don't need to be seduced." She arched up to him, offering her mouth, her body, herself.

"Let's see."

He covered her mouth with his, softly, dipping in when her lips trembled open. Under his hands, hers flexed, and gripped hard. How often had he loved her? It hadn't been long since they'd met, but he couldn't count the number of times he'd let his body take control, go wild with hers.

This time, he'd make love to her with his mind.

"I love your shoulders," he murmured, taking his mouth from hers for a slow exploration of the curve. "Soft, strong, smooth."

With his teeth, he caught the thin strap of her dress, tugged it down until there was nothing between him and flesh. Warmth, her taste, her scent, were all warmth. Absorbing them, he trailed his tongue over her shoulder, along the elegant line of throat, down again until the other strap gave way.

"And this spot here." He rubbed his lips just above the silk that curved over her breast. Teasingly, devastatingly, he dampened the skin under the silk with his tongue until her body moved restlessly beneath his. "You should relax and enjoy, Natalie. I'm going to be a while."

"I can't." The gentle brush of lips, the solid weight of him, were tormenting her. "Kiss me again."

"My pleasure."

There was a flicker of heat this time, bright

and hot, before he banked the fires again. She moaned, straining against him, wanting release, craving the torture. He made the choice for her, kissing her with a focused intensity until her fingers went limp and her rushed breathing slowed and thickened.

Smoke. She could all but smell it. She was rising up on clouds of it, weightless, helpless, unable to do more than float and sigh when his mouth left hers to trail down again. A gentle nip at the jaw, and then light, slow kisses down her throat, her shoulders.

His body shifted downward, his hands still covering hers. Inch by inch, he tasted her, nudging the silk down. She felt his hair brush her breast, then his mouth traveling around the curve, nuzzling at the sensitive underside. His tongue slid over her nipple, shooting an ache down to her center. Then he caught the peak between his teeth, making her moan his name, and her body began to throb to a low, primitive beat.

He wanted her to absorb him, and all the pleasure he could give her. Her eyes were closed, her lips just parted. And much too tempting. He needed to taste them again, and when he did, he let himself sink into the texture, the flavor.

Time spun out.

There was power here, in tenderness. He'd never felt it before, not in himself, and certainly not for anyone else. But for her he had a bottomless well of tenderness, of soft, sumptuous kisses, of endless sighs.

He took his hands from hers to shrug out of his shirt, to feel the thrill of his flesh against her flesh. Sliding smooth, building heat. With a murmur of approval, he slipped his hand through the slit of her skirt, lightly caressing, teasing the edge of some frilly something she wore beneath.

He flicked open a button, then two, then the third, fascinated by the way the material slid and parted under his hands. Nuzzling along her bared hip, he fought back a sudden, vicious urge to take when her hands brushed, then pressed, at his shoulders.

More, he promised himself. There was more.

For his own pleasure, he slipped the silk aside. And found more.

Beneath she wore a fancy of silk and lace, the same color as the dress that pooled beside them. Strapless, it hugged her breasts, rode high up her hips. Letting out a long breath, he sat back on his heels and toyed with one lacy garter.

"Natalie."

Weak…she was so gloriously weak she could barely open her eyes. When she did, she saw only him, the firelight teasing the red out of his dark hair, his eyes nearly black. She reached out, her arm heavy, nearly boneless. He merely took her hand, and kissed it.

"I wanted to tell you how happy I am you're in the lingerie business."

Her lips curved. She nearly managed a laugh before, with one quick flick, he detached the first garter. She could only utter a helpless moan.

"And how beautiful you look." Flick went the second garter. "Modeling your own products." With his eyes on hers, he rolled the stocking down thigh and knee and calf.

Her vision hazed. She could feel him. Oh, God, she could feel him—every brush of fingertip and mouth. Surrender had come gliding through her like a shadow, and had left her completely vulnerable. Whatever he wanted. Anything he wanted, she would give, as long as he never stopped touching her.

There was the low, steady heat from the fire. It was nothing, nothing, compared to the slow burn he had kindled inside her. As if down a long, velvet-lined tunnel, she could hear the music still. A quiet backdrop to her own trembling breathing. The scent of flowers and candle wax, the taste of him and the wine that lingered on her tongue, all melded together into one stunning intoxication.

Then he slipped a finger under the lace-edged hem, sliding it slowly toward, and then into, the heat.

She erupted. Her body quaked and reared. His name burst from her lips, even as the staggering pleasure careened through her system. She was wrapped around him as the power of the climax built in force, then echoed away and left her drained.

She wanted to tell him she was empty, had to be empty. But he was peeling away the silk and lace, exposing her with those clever fingers, swallowing whatever words she might have spoken with that relentlessly patient mouth.

"I want to fill you, Natalie." His hands weren't as steady as they had been, but he laid her gently back on the carpet so that he could tug off his clothes. "All of you. With all of me."

While the blood pounded in his ears, he began a slow journey up her legs, stoking the fires again, waiting, watching, for that moment before she would flash again.

He felt her body tense, saw the power of what was to come flicker over her face. Even as she cried out, he was inside her.

It was almost painful to hold himself back. And it was very sweet. Seeing her heavy eyes open, seeing the glaze of pleasure cloud them as he fought to keep from racing for the finish.

Swamped by a swirl of sensations, all but suffocating in the layers of them, she groped for his hands. When their fingers locked again, her heart was ready to burst. Her eyes stayed open and looked on his as each thrust rocked them, pushed them closer.

Then she was cartwheeling off the edge, reeling, tumbling free. His mouth came to hers, his lips forming her name as he leapt with her.

Twice on the elevator ride to her office the next morning, Natalie caught herself singing. Both times, she cleared her throat, shifted her briefcase from hand to hand and pretended not to notice the speculative looks of her fellow passengers.

So what? she thought as the elevator climbed.

She felt like singing. She felt like dancing. So what? She was in love.

And what was wrong with that? she asked herself as the elevator stopped to let off passengers on the thirty-first floor. Everyone was entitled to be in love, to feel as though their feet would never touch the ground again, to know the air had never smelled sweeter, the sun had never shone brighter.

It was wonderful to be in love. So wonderful, she wondered why she'd never tried it before.

Because there'd never been Ry before, she thought, and grinned.

How foolish she'd been to panic when she realized what she felt for Ry. How cowardly and ridiculous to be afraid, even for a moment, of loving.

If it made a woman vulnerable, comical, if it dazed and baffled her, what was wrong with that? Love should make you feel giddy and strong and soft-headed. She'd just never realized it before.

Humming to herself, she stepped out of the elevator on her floor and all but waltzed toward her office.

"Good morning, Ms. Fletcher." Maureen glanced surreptitiously at her clock. It wasn't up to her to point out that the boss was late. Even three minutes late was a precedent for Natalie Fletcher.

"Good morning, Maureen." She all but sang it, and thrust out a clutch of daffodils.

"Oh, thank you. They're lovely."

"Everyone should have daffodils this morning. Absolutely everyone." Natalie shook back her hair, scattering raindrops. "It's a gorgeous day, isn't it?"

Drizzling and chilly was what it was, but Maureen found herself grinning back. "Absolutely a classic spring morning. You've got a conference call scheduled for ten o'clock. Atlanta, Chicago."

"I know."

"And Ms. Marks was hoping you could fit her in afterward."

"Fine."

"Oh, and you're due at the flagship at 11:15, right after your 10:30 with Mr. Hawthorne."

"No problem."

"You have a lunch with—"

"I'll be there," Natalie called out, and swung into her office.

For the first time in recent memory, Natalie bypassed the coffeepot. She didn't need caffeine to pump through her blood. It was already swimming. She hung up her coat, set her briefcase aside, then moved to the office safe behind her favorite abstract print.

Taking out a pair of disks, she went to her desk to draft a brief memo to Deirdre.

An hour later, she was elbow-deep in work, making hasty notes as she juggled information and requests from three of her branches on the conference call.

"I'll fax authorization for that within the hour," she promised Atlanta. "Donald, see if you can squeeze out the time to go to the flagship with me—11:15. We can have our meeting on the way."

"I've got an ll:30 with Marketing," he told her. "Let me see if I can push it to after lunch."

"I'd appreciate it. I'd like tear sheets of all the ads and newspaper articles in Chicago. You can fax copies, but I'd like you to overnight the originals. I'll be checking in with L.A. and Dallas this afternoon, and we'll have a full report for all branches by end of day tomorrow."

She sat back, let out a long breath. "Gentlemen, synchronize your watches and alert the troops. 10:00 a.m., Saturday. Coast to coast."

After she closed the conference, Natalie pressed her buzzer. "Maureen, let Deirdre know

I'm free for about twenty minutes. Oh, and buzz Melvin for me."

"He's in the field, Ms. Fletcher."

"Oh, right." Annoyed with her lapse, Natalie glanced at her watch, calculated time. "I'll see if I can catch him at the plant later this afternoon. Leave a memo on his voice mail that I should be by around three."

"Yes, ma'am."

"After you buzz Deirdre, get me the head of shipping at the new warehouse."

"Right away."

By the time Deirdre knocked on the door and stepped in, Natalie was tapping at the keys on her desk computer. "Yes, I see that." Phone tucked at her ear, she gestured Deirdre to a seat. "Put a trace on that shipment. I want it in Atlanta no later than 9:00 a.m. tomorrow." She nodded, tapped. "Let me know as soon as it's located. Thanks."

She hung up, brushed a stray hair from her cheek. "There's always a glitch near zero hour."

Deirdre's brow wrinkled. "Bad?"

"No, just a slight delay on a shipment. Even without it, Atlanta's well stocked for the opening. But I don't want them to run low. Coffee?"

"No, I've already burned a hole in my stomach

lining, thanks. Or you have." She aimed a steely look at her boss. "Bonuses."

"Bonuses," Natalie agreed. "I have the percentages I want you to work with right here. Salary ratios, and so forth." She smiled a little. "I figured you wouldn't be wondering about how best to murder me if I did the preliminaries."

"Wrong."

Now Natalie laughed. "Deirdre, do you know why I value you so highly?"

"Nope."

"You have a mind like a calculator. The bonuses were earned, and I also consider them a good investment. Incentive to keep up the pace during the weeks ahead. There's usually a dip after the initial sales in a new business, both in profit and in labor. I think this will keep that dip from becoming a dive."

"That's all very well in theory," Deirdre began.

"Let's make it reality. And since it's basically a standard ratio across the board, I'd like you to hand the problem over to your assistant. That way you can concentrate on running the audit."

Still smiling, she handed over the disks, and her memo. "A great deal of what you'll need to run will be parallel with tax preparation. Take whatever time, and however many bodies in Accounting, you feel you'll need."

With a grimace, Deirdre accepted the disk. "You know why I value you so highly, Natalie?"

"Nope."

"Because there's no budging you, and you give impossible orders with such reasonableness."

"It's a gift," Natalie agreed. "You might want these hard copies."

Deirdre rose, hefting the file. "Thanks a lot."

"Anytime." She glanced up with a smile as Donald poked his head in the door.

"I'm clear until 12:30," he told her.

"Great. We'll head out now. Take your time," Natalie repeated to Deirdre as she crossed to the closet for her coat. "As long as I have the first figures on this quarter's profit and loss, and the totals from each department, by the end of next week."

Deirdre rolled her eyes at Donald. "Reasonably impossible." She set the disks on top of the file. "You're next," she warned him.

"Don't let her scare you, Donald. She's just gearing up to pit black ink against red." Natalie sailed through the door. "Just make sure the black wins."

"Quite a mood she's in," Donald murmured to Deirdre.

"She's flying, all right." Deirdre stared down at the files. "Let's hope we can keep it that way."

"Perfect, isn't it?" Content after their visit to the store, Natalie stretched out her legs in the back of the car, while her driver threaded through the lunch-hour traffic. "You'd never know there was a fire."

"A hell of a job," Donald agreed. "And the window treatment's spectacular. The salesclerks are going to be run ragged come Saturday."

"I'm counting on it." She touched a hand to his arm. "A lot of it's your doing, Donald. We never would have gotten off the ground like this without you, especially after the warehouse."

"Damage control." He brushed off her thanks with a shrug. "In six months we'll barely remember we had damage to control. And the profits will bring a smile even to Deirdre's face." He was counting on it.

"That would be a real coup."

"Just drop me off at the next corner," he told the driver. "The restaurant's only a couple of doors down."

"I appreciate you making time to go with me."

"No problem. Seeing the flagship back in shape made my day. It wasn't pleasant visualizing the office torn up like that. That wonderful antique desk ruined. The replacement's stunning, by the way."

"I had it shipped out from Colorado," Natalie said absently, as something niggled at her brain. "I had it in storage."

"Well, it's perfect." He patted her hand as the car swung to the curb.

She waved him off, then settled back, dissatisfied, when the car merged back into traffic. Then, with a shrug, she gauged the traffic, the distance to her lunch meeting, and decided she had time for one quick phone call.

Ry answered himself on the third ring. "Arson. Piasecki."

"Hi." The pleasure of hearing his voice wiped out everything else. "Your secretary's out?"

"Lunch."

"And you're having yours at your desk."

He glanced down at the sandwich he had yet to touch. "Yeah. More or less." He shifted, making his chair squeak. "Where are you?"

"Looks like Twelfth and Hyatt, heading east, toward the Menagerie."

"Ah." The Menagerie, he thought. High-class. No tuna on wheat for lunch there. He could see her, ordering designer water and a salad with every leaf called a different name. "Look, Legs, about tonight—"

"I was thinking about that. Maybe you could meet me at the Goose Neck." She rolled her shoulders. "I have a feeling I'm going to want to unwind."

He rubbed a hand over his chin. "I, ah… Come by my place instead. Okay?"

"Your place?" This was new. She'd stopped wondering why he'd never taken her there.

"Yeah. About seven, seven-thirty."

"All right. Do you want me to pick up something for dinner?"

"No, I'll take care of it. See you." He hung up and sat back in his chair. He was going to have to take care of a lot of things.

He picked up Chinese. It was nearly seven when Ry carried the little white cartons up the two flights to his apartment. He took a good look around while he did.

It wasn't a dump. Unless, of course, you compared it with Natalie's glossy building. There was no graffiti on the walls, but the walls were thin. As he climbed the steps, Ry could hear the muted sounds of televisions playing, children squabbling. The steps themselves were worn down in the centers from the passage of countless feet.

As he turned onto the second floor, he heard a door slam beneath him.

"All right, all right. I'll go get the damn beer myself."

Lip curled, Ry unlocked his door. Yeah, he thought. It was a real class joint. There was a definite scent of garlic in the hall. Courtesy of his neighbor, he assumed. The woman was always cooking up pots of pasta.

He let himself in, flicked on the lights and studied the room.

It was clean. A little dusty, maybe. He barely spent enough time in it to mess it up. It had been nearly three weeks since he'd spent a night there. The sofa that folded out into a bed needed recovering. It wasn't something he'd noticed before, or would have bothered with. But now the faded blue upholstery annoyed him.

He walked past it, taking about half a dozen steps into the alcove that served as his kitchen. He got out a beer and popped the top. The walls needed painting, too, he decided, chugging the beer as he looked around. And the bare floors could have used a carpet.

But it served him well enough, didn't it? he thought grimly. He didn't need fancy digs. Just a couple of rooms a short hop from the office. He'd been content here for nearly a decade. That was enough for anyone.

But it wasn't enough, couldn't be enough, for Natalie.

She didn't belong here. He knew it. And he'd asked her to come to prove it to both of them.

The night before had been a revelation to him. That she could make him feel the way she'd made him feel. That she could make him forget, as he'd forgotten, that there was anything or anyone on the planet except the two of them.

It wasn't fair to either of them to go on this way. The longer he let it drift, the more he needed her. And the more he needed, the more difficult it would be to let her walk away.

His divorce hadn't hurt him. Oh, a couple of twinges, he thought now. Plenty of regrets. But no real pain. Not the deep-rooted, searing kind of pain he was already feeling at the thought of living without Natalie.

He could keep her. There was a good chance he could keep her. The physical thing between them was outrageously intense. Even if it faded by half, it would still be stronger than anything he'd ever experienced before.

And he was well aware of his effect on her.

He could hold her with sex alone. It might be enough for her. But he'd understood when he awakened beside her this morning that it wasn't enough for him.

No, it wasn't enough, not when he'd started to imagine white picket fences, kids in the yard—the kind of things that went with marriage, permanence, a lifetime.

That hadn't been the deal, he reminded himself. And he had no right to change the rules, to expect her to settle. He'd already proven he wasn't any good at marriage, and that had been with someone from his own neighborhood, his own lifestyle. No way was he going to fit in with Natalie, and the fact that he wanted to, needed to, scared the hell out of him.

Worse than that, even worse, was the idea that she would turn him down cold if he asked her to try.

He wanted all of her. Or nothing. So it made

sense, didn't it, to push her out before he got in any deeper? And he would do it here, right here, where the differences between them would slap her between the eyes.

At the knock on his door, he carried his beer over to answer it.

It was just as he'd thought. She stood in the hallway, slim, golden, an exotic fish completely out of water. She smiled at him, leaning up to kiss him.

"Hi."

"Hi. Come on in. No trouble finding the place?"

"No." She skimmed her sweep of hair back, looking around. "I took a cab."

"Good thinking. If you left that fancy car on the street around here, there'd be nothing left but the door handles when you went back out. Want a beer?"

"No." Interested, she wandered over to the window.

"Not much of a view," he said, knowing she was looking out at the face of the next building.

"Not much," she agreed. "It's still raining," she added and slipped out of her coat. She smiled when she spotted another of his basketball trophies. "MVP," she murmured, reading the plaque. "Impressive. I say I can outscore you nine times out of ten."

"I wasn't fresh." He turned into the kitchen. "I don't have any wine."

"That's okay. Mmm…Chinese." She opened one of the cartons he'd set on the counter, and sniffed. "I'm starved. All I had was a stingy salad for lunch. I've been all over the city today, nailing down details for Saturday. Where are the plates?" Very much at home, she opened a cabinet herself. "I'm really going to have to make a sweep of the branches next week. I was thinking—" She broke off when she turned back and found him staring at her. "What?"

"Nothing," he muttered, and took the plates out of her hands.

She wasn't supposed to stride right in and start chattering, he thought, and dumped food on a plate. She was supposed to see how wrong it was, right from the start. She was supposed to make it easy on him.

"Damn it, do you see where you are?" He whirled on her, taking her back a step.

She blinked. "Ah…in the kitchen?"

"Look around you." Incensed, he took her by the arm and dragged her into the next room. "Look around. This is it. This is the way I live. This is the way I am."

"All right." She pushed his hand away, because his fingers hurt. Trying to oblige, she took another survey of the room. It was spartan, masculine in its very simplicity. Small, she noted, but not crowded. A table across the room held framed snapshots of a family she hoped to get a closer look at.

"It could use some color," she decided after a moment.

"I'm not asking for decorating advice," he snapped out.

There was something under the anger in his tone, something final, that had her heart stuttering. Very slowly, she turned back to him. "What are you asking for?"

Cursing, he spun into the kitchen for his beer. If she was going to look at him with that confused, wounded look in her eyes, he was a dead man. So, he would have to be cruel, and he would have to be quick. He sat on the arm of the couch, and tipped back his beer.

"Let's get real here, Natalie. You and I started this thing because we were hot for each other."

She could feel the warmth drain out of her cheeks, leaving them cold and stiff. But she kept her eyes level, and her voice steady. "Yes, that's right."

"Things happened fast. The sex, the investigation. Things got tangled up."

"Did they?"

His mouth was dry, and the beer wasn't helping. "You're a beautiful woman. I wanted you. You had a problem. It was my job to fix it for you."

"Which you did," she said carefully.

"For the most part. The cops'll track down whoever was paying Clarence. Until they do, you've got to be careful. But things are pretty much under control. On that level."

"And on the personal level?"

He frowned down into the bottle. "I figure it's time to step back, take a clearer look."

Natalie's legs were trembling. She locked her knees to stop it. "Are you dumping me, Ry?"

"I'm saying we've got to look behind the way things are in bed. The way you are." He lifted his gaze. "The way I'm not. We've got plenty of heat, Natalie. The problem with that is, you get blinded by the smoke. Time to clear the air, that's all."

"I see." She wouldn't beg. Nor would she cry, not in front of him. Not when he was looking at her so coolly, his voice so casual as he cut out her heart. She wondered if he'd been so gentle, so loving and sweet, the night before because he'd already decided to break things off.

"Well, I suppose you've cleared it." Despite her resolve, her vision blurred, the lamplight refracting in the tears that trembled much too close to the surface.

The minute her eyes filled, he was on his feet. "Don't."

"I won't. Believe me, I won't." But the first tear spilled over as she turned toward the door. "I appreciate you not doing this in a public place." She clamped a hand over the doorknob. Her fingers were numb, she realized. She couldn't even feel them.

"Natalie."

"I'm all right." To prove it to both of them, she turned to face him, her head up. "I'm not a child, and this isn't the first relationship I've had that hasn't worked. It is the first time for something, though, and you're entitled to know it. You jerk." She sniffed, and wiped a tear away. "I've never been in love with anyone before, but I fell in love with you. I hate you for it."

She yanked open the door and dashed out without her coat.

Chapter 11

For ten minutes, Ry paced the room, convincing himself he'd done the right thing for both of them. Sure, she'd be a little hurt. Her pride was bruised. He hadn't exactly been a diplomat.

For the next ten, he worked on convincing himself that she hadn't meant what she'd said. That parting shot had been just that. A weapon hurled to hurt as she'd been hurt.

She wasn't in love with him. She couldn't be. Because if she was, then he was the world's biggest idiot.

Oh, God. He was the world's biggest idiot.

He snatched up her coat, forgot his own, and raced downstairs and out into the rain.

He'd left his car at the station, and cursed himself for it. Praying for a cab, he loped to the corner, then to the next, working his way across town.

His impatience cost him more time than a simple wait would have. By the time he hailed an empty cab, he was twelve blocks from his home and soaking wet.

The cab fought its way through rain and traffic, creeping along, then sprinting, creeping, then sprinting, until Ry tossed a fistful of money at the driver and leapt out.

He'd have made better time on foot.

Nearly an hour had passed by the time he arrived at Natalie's door. He didn't bother to knock, but used the key she hadn't thought to demand back from him.

There was no welcome this time, no cozy sense of coming home. He knew the minute he stepped inside that she wasn't there. Denying it, he called out for her and began a dripping search through the apartment.

So he'd wait, he told himself. She'd come home sooner or later, and he'd be there. Make things right again somehow. He'd grovel if he had to, he decided, pacing from the living room to the bedroom.

She'd probably gone to her office. Maybe he should go there. He could call. He could send a telegram. He could do something.

Good God, the woman was in love with him, and he'd used both hands to shove her out the door.

He dropped to the side of the bed and snatched up the phone. It was then that he saw the note, hastily scrawled, on the nightstand.

Atlanta—National—8:25

National, he thought. National Airlines. The airport.

Ry was out of the apartment and harassing the doorman for a cab in three minutes flat.

He missed her plane by less than five.

"No, Inspector Piasecki, I don't know precisely when Ms. Fletcher expects to return." Cautiously, Maureen smiled. The man looked wild, as though he'd spent a very rough night in his clothes. Things were upended enough, with the boss's sudden trip, without her having to face down a madman at 9:00 a.m.

"Where is she?" Ry demanded. He'd very nearly caught the next flight out to Atlanta the night before, but then it had occurred to him that he didn't have a clue where to find her.

"I'm sorry, Inspector. I'm not allowed to give you that information. I will be happy to relay any message you might have when Ms. Fletcher calls in."

"I want to know where she is," Ry said between his teeth.

Maureen gave serious thought to calling Security. "It's company policy—"

He gave a one-word assessment of company policy and pulled out his ID. "Do you see this? I'm in charge of the arson investigation. I've got information Ms. Fletcher requires immediately. Now, if you don't let me know where to reach her, I'll have to go to my superiors."

He let that hang, and hoped.

Torn, Maureen bit her lip. It was true Ms. Fletcher had ordered her specifically not to divulge her itinerary. It was also true that during the harried phone call the night before, nothing had been mentioned specifically about information from Inspector Piasecki. And if it was something to do with the fires…

"She's staying at the Ritz-Carlton, Atlanta."

Before she'd finished the sentence, Ry was out the door. It was best, he decided, if a man was going to whimper, to do it in private.

Fifteen minutes later, he burst into his office, startling his secretary, and slammed the door behind him. "Ritz-Carlton, Atlanta. Get them on the phone."

"Yes, sir."

He paced his office, muttering to himself, until she signaled him. "Natalie Fletcher," he barked into the phone. "Connect me."

"Yes, sir. One moment, please."

One endless moment, while the line whispered, then began to ring. Ry let out a long, relieved breath when he heard Natalie's voice at the other end.

"Natalie—what the hell are you doing in Atlanta? I need to—" Then he could only swear as the phone clicked loudly in his ear. "Damn it all to hell and back, get that number for me again."

Wide-eyed, his secretary hurriedly placed the call.

Calm, Ry ordered himself. He knew how to be calm in the face of fire and death and misery. Surely he could be calm now. But when the phone continued to ring and he pictured her coolly looking out the window of her hotel room and ignoring it, he nearly ripped the receiver out of the wall.

"Call the airport," Ry ordered while his secretary goggled at him. "Book me on the next available flight to Atlanta."

She was gone when he got there.

He couldn't believe it. More than ten hours after his rushed departure, Ry was back in Urbana. Alone. He hadn't even managed to see her. He'd spent hours on planes, more time chasing her around Atlanta, from her hotel to the downtown branch of Lady's Choice, back to her hotel, to the airport. Each time he'd missed her by inches.

It was, he thought as he trudged up the stairs to his apartment, as if she'd known he was behind her. He dropped down on the couch, rubbing his hands over his face.

He had no choice but to wait.

"I'm so glad to see you." Althea Grayson Nightshade smiled as she rubbed a hand over her mountain of a belly.

"That goes double." Natalie laughed. "Literally. How are you feeling?"

"Oh, like a cross between the Goodyear blimp and Moby Dick."

"Neither of them ever looked so good." It was true, Natalie mused. Pregnancy had only enhanced Althea's considerable beauty. Her eyes were gold, her skin was dewy, her hair was a fiery cascade to her shoulders.

"I'm fat, but I'm healthy." Althea's lips twitched. "Colt's been a demon about seeing that I eat right, sleep enough, exercise, rest. He even typed up a daily schedule. Mr. Play-It-By-Ear went into a tailspin when he found out we were expecting."

"The nursery's wonderful." Natalie wandered the sunny mint-and-white room, running her fingers over the antique crib, the fussy dotted-swiss curtains.

"I'll be glad when it's filled. Any time now," Althea said with a sigh. "I feel great, really, but I swear, this has been the longest pregnancy in recorded history. I want to see my baby, damn it." She stopped and laughed at herself. "Listen to me. I never thought I'd want children, much less be itching to change the first diaper."

Intrigued, Natalie looked over her shoulder. Althea sat in a rocking chair, a small, poorly knit blanket in her hands. "No? You never wanted to be a mom?"

"Not with the job and my background." She shrugged. "Didn't figure I was cut out for it. Then along comes Nightshade, and then this." She patted her belly. "Maybe gestating isn't my natural milieu, but I've loved every minute of it. Now I'm antsy to get on to the nurturing. Can you see me," she said with a laugh, "sitting here, rocking a baby?"

"Yes, I can." Natalie came back, crouched, and took Althea's hands. "I envy you, Thea. So much. To have someone who loves you, to make a baby between you. Nothing else is as important." Defenses crumbled. Her eyes filled.

"Oh, honey, what is it?"

"What else?" Disgusted with herself, Natalie straightened.

"A man."

"A jerk." She fought back the tears and stuffed her hands in her pockets.

"Would this jerk be an arson investigator?" Althea smiled a little when Natalie scowled at her. "News travels, even to Denver. The fact is, your family and Colt and I have been biting our tongues, trying not to ask what you're doing out here."

"I explained. I'm siting. I want to open another branch here. I was traveling, anyway."

"Instead of being in Urbana for your opening."

She resented that, laid the blame for it right at Ry's doorstep. "I was in Dallas for the opening there. Each of my branches is of equal importance to me."

"Yeah, and word is it was a smash."

"The tallies for the first week's sales look promising."

"So why aren't you back home, basking in it?" Althea inclined her head. "The jerk?"

"I'm entitled to a little time before I… Well, yes," she admitted. "The jerk. He dumped me."

"Oh, come on. Cilla said the guy was crazy about you."

"We were good in bed," Natalie said flatly, then pressed her lips together. "I made the mistake of falling in love with him. A real first for me. And he broke my heart."

"I'm sorry." Concerned, Althea pushed herself out of the chair.

"I'll get over it." Natalie squeezed Althea's offered hands. "It's just that I've never felt this way about anyone. I didn't know I could. I've managed to get through my whole life without being hurt like this. Then, *pow.* It's like being cut into very small pieces," she murmured. "I just haven't been able to put them all back together yet."

"Well, he's not worth it," Althea said loyally.

"I wish that were true. It'd be easier. He's a wonderful man, tough, sweet, dedicated." She moved her shoulders restlessly. "He didn't mean to hurt me. He's called several times while I've been on the road."

"He must want to apologize, to make things up with you."

"Do you think I'd give him the chance?" Natalie's chin angled. "I'm not taking his calls. I'm not taking anything from him. He can send me flowers all over the country, for all the difference it would make."

"He sends you flowers." A smile was beginning to lurk around the corners of Althea's mouth.

"Daffodils. Every time I turn around, I'm getting a bunch of idiotic daffodils." She set her teeth. "Does he think I'm going to fall for that again?"

"Probably."

"Well, I'm not. One broken heart's enough for me. More than enough."

"Maybe you should go back, let him beg. Then kick him in the teeth." Althea winced at the twinge. The third one, she noted with a glance at her watch, in the past half hour.

"I'm thinking about it. But until I'm ready, I'm not—" Natalie broke off. "What is it? Are you all right?"

"Yeah." Althea let out a long breath. This twinge was lasting longer. "You know, I think I could be going into labor."

"What?" The blood drained out of Natalie's face. "Now? Sit. Sit down, for God's sake. I'll get Colt."

"Maybe I will." Gingerly Althea lowered herself back into the chair. "Maybe you'd better."

Deirdre was glad she'd decided to take the work home with her. The miserable cold she'd picked up from somewhere was hanging on like a leech. At least she could take her mind off her stuffy head and scratchy throat with work.

She sniffed disinterestedly at the cup of instant chicken soup she'd zapped in the microwave and indulged herself with the hot toddy instead. Nothing like a good shot of whiskey to make a cup of tea sit up and sing.

If she was lucky, very lucky, she'd have the cold on the run and the preliminary figures in before Natalie got back from Denver.

She took another hefty slug of the spiked tea and tapped keys. She stopped, frowned, and adjusted her glasses.

That couldn't be right, she thought, and tapped more keys. No way in hell could that be right. Her mouth became drier, and a thin line of sweat rolled down her back that had nothing to do with the slight fever she was fighting.

She sat back and took a couple of easy breaths. It was simply a mistake, she assured herself. She'd find the discrepancy and fix it. That was all.

But it didn't take much longer for her to realize it wasn't a mistake. Or an accident.

It was a quarter of a million dollars. And it was gone.

She snatched up the phone, and rapidly dialed. "Maureen. Deirdre Marks."

"Ms. Marks, you sound dreadful."

"I know. Listen, I need to talk to Natalie, right away."

"Who doesn't?"

"It's urgent, Maureen. She's with her brother, right? Let me have the number."

"I can't do that, Ms. Marks."

"It's urgent, I tell you."

"I understand, but she's not there. Her plane left Denver an hour ago. She's on her way home."

A son. Althea and Colt had a son, a tiny and beautiful boy. It had taken Althea twelve hard hours to push him into the world, and he'd come out howling.

Natalie remembered it now as her plane traveled east. It had been a thrill to be allowed in the birthing room, to support Colt when he was ready to climb the walls, to watch him and Althea work together to welcome that new life.

She hadn't wept until it was over, until she'd left Colt and Althea nuzzling their new son. Boyd had left the hospital with her. He'd either been too deep in the memories of his own children's births or had sensed her mood. Either way, he hadn't badgered her.

Now she was going home, because there was work to do. And because it was cowardly to keep jumping from city to city because she was hurt.

It had been a good trip. Professionally successful. Personally soothing. She was going to give some thought to moving back to Colorado. She'd found an excellent site. And a new branch in Denver would benefit from her personal touch.

If the move would have the added benefit of escape, whose business was it but hers?

She would have to wait, of course, until they had unearthed whoever had paid Clarence Jacoby. If it was indeed one of her people in Urbana, that person had to be weeded out. Once that was done, Donald could take over that office.

It would be a simple matter. Donald had the talent. From a business standpoint, the change would be little more than having him move from his office to hers, his desk to hers.

Desk, she thought, frowning. There was something odd about the desk. Not her desk, she realized all at once. The desk that had been damaged at the flagship.

He'd known about that. Her heart began to thud uncomfortably. How had Donald known the desk in the manager's office was an antique? How had he known specifically that it had been damaged?

Cautiously she began to think over the details, recalling her movements from the time of the second fire to the day she and Donald had visited the flagship. He hadn't been in the office there since it had been decorated. At least not to her knowledge. So how could he have known the desks had been switched?

Because he'd been there. That was all, she tried to assure herself. He'd swung by at some point and hadn't mentioned it. It made sense, more sense than believing he had had something to do with the fires.

Yet he'd been at the warehouse the morning after it had burned. Early, she remembered. Had she called him? She couldn't be sure, didn't recall. He could have heard about it on the news. Had there been reports that early? Detailed reports? She wasn't sure about that, either, and it worried her.

Why should he do something so drastic to harm a business he was an integral part of? she wondered. What possible motive could there be for him to want to see stock and equipment destroyed?

Stock, equipment, and, she thought on a jolt of alarm, records. There'd been records at the warehouse, and at the flagship—at the point of the fire's origin.

Determined to keep calm, she thought of the files she'd given Deirdre, of the copies still in the safe at her office. She'd check them herself the minute she landed, just to ease her mind.

She was wrong about Donald, of course. She had to be wrong.

* * *

She was late. It was a hell of a thing, Ry thought as he paced the gate area at the airport, for a woman who was so fixated on being on time. Now, when he was all but jumping out of his skin, she had to be late.

It didn't matter that the plane was late, and she just happened to be on it. He took it as a personal affront.

If Maureen hadn't taken pity on him, he wouldn't have known she was coming back tonight. It grated a bit, to know that Natalie's secretary felt sorry for him. That she must have seen that he looked like a lovesick mongrel.

Even the men at the station were starting to talk about him behind his back.

Oh, he knew it, all right. The mutters, the snickers, the pitying looks. Anybody with eyes in his head could see that the past ten days had been torment for him.

He'd made a mistake, damn it. One little mistake, and she'd paid him back. Big-time.

They were just going to have to put that behind them.

He clutched the daffodils, paced, and felt like a fool. His heart took one frantic leap when her flight was announced.

294 Night Smoke

He saw her, and his palms began to sweat.

She saw him, turned sharply left, and kept walking.

"Natalie." He caught up with her in two strides. "Welcome home."

"Go to hell."

"I've been there for the past ten days. I don't like it." It wasn't hard to keep up with her, since she was wearing heels. "Here."

She glanced down at the daffodils, cutting a scathing look up to his face. "You don't want me to tell you what you can do with those stupid flowers, do you?"

"You could have talked to me when I called."

"I didn't want to talk to you." Deliberately she swung into the closest ladies' room.

Ry gritted his teeth and waited.

She told herself she wasn't pleased that he was still there when she came out. Saying nothing, she quickened her pace toward the baggage-claim area.

"How was your trip?"

She snarled at him.

"Look, I'm trying to apologize here."

"Is that what you're doing?" With a toss of her head, she stepped onto the escalator heading down. "Save it."

"I screwed up. I'm sorry. I've been trying to tell you for days, but you won't take my calls."

"That should indicate something, Piasecki, even to someone of your limited intelligence."

"So," he continued, biting back hot words, "I'm here to pick you up, so we can talk."

"I've ordered a car."

"We canceled it. That is…" He had to choose his words carefully, with that icy look in her eyes freezing him. "I canceled it, when I found out you were coming in." No need to make Maureen fry with him, he decided. "So I'll give you a lift."

"I'll take a cab."

"Don't be so damn stubborn. I'll get tough if I have to," he muttered as they joined the throng at Baggage Claim. "I can have you up in a fireman's carry in two seconds. Embarrass the hell out of you. Either way, I'm driving you home."

She debated. He would embarrass her. There was no point in giving him the satisfaction. Nor was she going to tell him of her suspicions, not until she had something solid. Not until she had no choice but to deal with him on a professional level.

"I'm not going home. I need to go to the office."

"The office is closed. It's almost nine o'clock."

"I'm going to the office," she said flatly, and turned away from him.

"Fine. We'll talk at the office."

"That one." She pointed to a gray tweed Pullman. "And that one." A matching garment bag. "And that." Another Pullman.

"You didn't have time to pack all this before I got to your apartment that night."

Interested despite herself, she watched him heft cases. "I picked up luggage and clothes along the way."

"Enough for a damn modeling troupe," he muttered.

"I beg your pardon?" Her tone lowered the temperature in the terminal by ten degrees.

"Nothing. Your opening made a real splash," he continued as they walked out of the terminal.

"It met our expectations."

"You're getting write-ups in *Newsday* and *Business Week*." He shrugged when she looked at him. "I heard."

"And *Women's Wear Daily*," she added. "But who's counting?"

"I've been. It's great, Natalie, really. I'm happy for you. Proud of you." He set her luggage beside his car, and his limbs went weak. "God, I've missed you."

She stepped back, evading him, when he reached for her. He was not going to hurt her again, she promised herself. She would not allow it.

"Okay." Slowly, stunned by the ache that one quick rejection caused, he lifted his hands, palms out. "I had that coming. I've got plenty coming. I'll give you the chance to take all the shots you want."

"I'm not interested in fighting with you," she said wearily. "I've had a long trip. I'm too tired to fight with you."

"Let me take you home, Natalie."

"I'm going to the office." She stepped back and waited for him to unlock the car. Once inside, she sat back and shut her eyes. She just sighed when Ry laid the bright yellow flowers in her lap.

"They, ah, haven't gotten any more out of Clarence," he said, hoping to chip at the wall she'd erected between them.

"I know." She couldn't think about her suspicions yet. "I've kept in touch."

"You moved around fast."

"I had a lot of ground to cover."

"Yeah." He dug out money for the parking attendant. "I got the picture, after I chased you around Atlanta."

She opened her eyes then. "Excuse me?"

"I couldn't get a damn cab," he muttered. "You must have hooked one the minute you walked out of my apartment."

"Yes, I did."

"Figures. I'm running the marathon to your apartment, then you're gone when I get there. I see the note, figure the airport, and get there in time to see your plane take off."

She felt herself softening, and stiffened. "Is that supposed to be my fault, Piasecki?"

"No, it's not your fault, damn it. It's my fault. But if you could have sat still in Atlanta for five minutes, we'd have settled this."

"We *have* settled it."

"Not by a long shot." Turning his head, he aimed a deadly look at her. "I hate it when people hang up on me."

"It was," she said with relish, "my pleasure."

"I might have strangled you for it when I got down there. If I could have caught you. 'No, Ms. Fletcher's at her shop.' Then I get to the shop, and it's 'Sorry, Ms. Fletcher's gone back to her hotel.' I get back to the hotel, and you've checked out. I get to the airport and you're in the sky. I spent hours chasing my tail, trying to catch up with you."

She shrugged. She didn't want to be pleased, but she couldn't prevent a little frisson of pleasure at the frustration in his voice. "Don't expect an apology." Still, she gathered up the flowers to keep them from sliding from her lap when he braked.

"I'm trying to give *you* one."

"There's no need. I've had time to think about it, and I've decided you were absolutely right. I don't like the style you used, but the bottom line rings true. We had some interesting chemistry. That's all."

"We had a lot more than that. We've got more than that. Natalie—"

"This is my stop." Forgetting her luggage, she bolted out of the car. By the time Ry had parked, illegally, she was waiting for the security guard to open the front door of her building.

"Damn it, Natalie, would you hold still?"

"I have work. Good evening, Ben."

"Ms. Fletcher. Working late?"

"That's right." She breezed past the guard, with Ry at her heels. "There's no need for you to come up with me, Ry."

"You said you loved me."

Ignoring the guard's speculative look, Natalie pressed the elevator button. "I got over it."

Panic spurted through him, freezing him in

place. He barely made it into the elevator before the doors shut in his face. "You did not."

"I know what I did, I know what I didn't." She jabbed the button for her floor. "It's all ego with you. You're causing a scene because I didn't come back when you called." She tossed her hair back. Her eyes were bright. Not with tears, he saw with some relief. But with anger. "Because I don't need you."

"It has nothing to do with ego. I was—" He couldn't admit he'd been scared, down-to-the-bone scared. "I was wrong," he said. That was hard enough, but at least it wasn't humiliating. "It was you—there in my place. I asked you to come because it was so obvious."

"What was obvious?"

"That it couldn't be real. I didn't see how it could be real. Who you are, the way you are. And me."

Her eyes sharpened, narrowed. "Am I following you here, Inspector? You dumped me because I didn't fit in with your apartment."

It didn't have to sound that stupid. His voice rose in defense. "With everything. With me. I can't give you…the things. The first time I remembered I should give you flowers once in a while, you looked at me like I'd clipped you on the jaw. I never take you anywhere. I don't think of it. You've got friends who live in mansions. And look, damn it, you've got diamonds in your ears right now." He tossed up his hands, as if that should explain everything. "Diamonds, for God's sake."

Her cheeks were hot now. She was all but radiating heat as she stepped toward him. "Is this about money? Is that it? You broke my heart over money?"

"No, it's about…things." How could he explain what made no sense at all anymore? "Natalie, let me touch you."

"The hell with you." She shoved him back, bounding through the elevator the minute the doors open. "You tossed me aside because you thought I wanted you to get me diamonds, or a mansion, or flowers?" Furious, she tossed the daffodils on the floor. "I can get my own diamonds, or anything else I want. What I wanted was you."

"Don't walk away. Don't." Swearing, he rushed after her. Somewhere down the long corridor, a phone rang. "Natalie." He grabbed her by the shoulders, spun her around. "I didn't think that, exactly."

She rammed her briefcase hard into his gut. "And you had the nerve to call me a snob."

Out of patience, he rammed her back against the wall. "It was wrong. It was stupid. *I* was stupid. What more do you want me to say? I wasn't thinking. I was just feeling."

"You hurt me."

"I know." He rested his brow on hers, tried to get his bearings. He could smell her, feel her, and the thought of losing her made him weak in the knees. "I'm sorry. I didn't know I could hurt you. I thought it was just me. I thought you'd walk."

"So you walked first."

He drew back a little. "Something like that."

"Coward." She jerked away. "Go away, Ry. Leave me alone. I have to think about this."

"You're still in love with me. I'm not going anywhere until you tell me."

"Then you'll have to wait, because I'm not ready to tell you anything." Phones were ringing. Wearily rubbing her temple, Natalie wondered who would be calling so long after hours. "I'm raw, don't you understand? I realized I loved you and had you break it off almost simultaneously. I'm not going to serve you my emotions on a platter."

"Then I'll give you mine," he said quietly. "I love you, Natalie."

Her heart swam into her eyes. "Damn you. *Damn* you! That's not fair."

"I can't be worried about fair." He stepped closer, and reached out to touch her hair. His hand froze when he saw the flicker of light at the end of the hall. It danced through the glass in a pattern he recognized too well. "Take the fire stairs down, now. Call Dispatch."

"What? What are you talking about?"

"Go," he repeated, and dashed down the hall. He could smell smoke now, and cursed it. Cursed himself for being so intent on his own needs that he'd missed it. He saw it, the crafty plume under the door that flowed out, sucked in.

"Oh, God. Ry."

She was right behind him. He had time to see the flames writhing behind the glass, time to judge. Then he turned, leapt and knocked Natalie to the ground as the window exploded. Lethal shards of glass rained over them.

Chapter 12

She felt pain, sharp and shocking, as her head thudded against the floor, and pinpricks of heat from the glass and flame. For a terrifying moment, she thought Ry was unconscious, or dead. His body was fully spread over hers, a shield protecting her from the worst of the blast.

Before she could even sob in the breath to scream his name, he was up and dragging her to her feet.

"Are you burned?"

She shook her head, aware only of the throbbing, and the smoke that was beginning to sting her eyes, her throat. She could barely see his face through it, but she saw the blood.

"Your face, your arm—you're bleeding."

But he wasn't listening. He had her hand vised in his, and was dragging her away from the flame. Even as they dashed down the hall, another window exploded. Fire roared out.

It surrounded them, golden and greedy, unbelievably hot. She screamed once as she saw it race along the floor, eating its way toward them, spitting like a hundred hungry snakes.

Panic gripped her, icy fingers clutching at her stomach, squeezing her throat, in taunting contrast to the heat pulsing around them. They were trapped, fire writhing on either side of them. Terrified, she fought him when he pushed her to the floor.

"Stay low." However grim his thoughts, his voice was calm. He gripped her hair in one hand to keep her face turned to his. He needed her to hold on to control.

"I can't breathe." The smoke was choking her, making her gasp for air and expel what little she had in gritty coughs.

"There's more air down here. We don't have much time." He was aware—too well aware—of how quickly the fire would reach them, how well it blocked their exit to the stairs. He had nothing with which to fight it.

If the fire didn't kill them, the smoke would, long before rescue could reach them.

"Get out of your coat."

"What?"

Her movements were already sluggish. He fought back panic and yanked her coat from her shoulders. "We're going through it."

"We can't." She couldn't even scream at the next explosion of glass, could only huddle, racked by coughing. Her mind was dull, stunned by smoke. She wanted only to lie down and draw in the precious air that still hovered just above the floor. "We'll burn. I don't want to die that way."

"You're not going to die." Tossing the coat over her head, he dragged her to her feet. When she staggered, he lifted her over his shoulder. He stood, fire lapping on both sides, a flaming sea around him. In seconds, the tidal wave would reach them, and they'd drown in it.

He gauged the distance and sprinted into the wave.

For an instant, they were in hell. Fire, heat, the roaring of its anger, the quick, ravenous licking of its tongues. For no more than two heartbeats—an eternity—flames engulfed them. He felt the hair on his hands singe, knew from the intense heat on his back and arms that his jacket would catch. He knew exactly what fire did to human flesh. He wouldn't allow it to have Natalie.

Then they were through it, and into a wall of smoke. Blinded, lungs straining, he groped for the fire door.

Instinctively he checked it for heat, thanked God, then shoved it open. Smoke was billowing up the stairwell, rising as if in a chimney that meant fire below, as well, but they didn't have a choice. Moving fast, he ripped the smoldering coat away from her and leaned her against the wall while he stripped off his own jacket.

The leather was burning, sluggishly.

Dazed by the smoke and teetering into shock, Natalie slid bonelessly to the floor.

"You're not giving up," he snapped at her as he hauled her back over his shoulder. "Hang on, damn it. Just hang on."

He streaked down the steps, one flight, then two, then a third. She was dead weight now, her head lolling, her arms limp. His eyes were watering from the smoke, the tears joining the river of sweat rolling down his face. The coughing that seized him felt as if it would shatter his ribs. All he knew was that he had to get her to safety.

He counted each level, keeping his mind focused. The smoke began to thin, and he began to hope.

She never stirred, not even when he tested the door at the lobby level, found it cool, and staggered through.

He heard the shouts, the sirens. His vision grayed as two firefighters rushed toward him.

"God almighty, Inspector."

"She needs oxygen." Still holding her, Ry shoved the offer of assistance aside and carried her outside, into clean air.

Lights were swirling. All the familiar sounds and scents and sights of a fire scene. Like a drunk, he weaved toward the closest engine.

"Oxygen," he ordered. "Now." Another coughing fit battered him as he laid her down.

Her face was black with soot, and her eyes were closed. He couldn't see if she was breathing, couldn't hear. Someone was shouting, raging, but he had no idea it was him. Hands pushed his own fumbling ones aside and fit an oxygen mask over Natalie's face.

"You need attention, Inspector."

"Keep away from me." He bent over her, searching for a pulse. Blood dripped down his arm and onto her throat. "Natalie. Please."

"Is she all right?" With tears streaming down her face, Deirdre dropped down beside him. "Is she going to be all right?"

"She's breathing," was all Ry could say. "She's breathing," he repeated, stroking her hair.

Mercifully, most of the next hour was a blur. He remembered climbing into the ambulance with her, holding her hand. Someone pressed oxygen on him, bound up his arm. They took her away the minute they hit the E.R. His panicked raging came out in hacking coughs.

Then the world turned upside down.

He found himself flat on his back on an examining table. When he tried to push himself upright, he was restrained.

"Just lie still." A small, gray-haired woman was scowling at him. "I like my stitches neat and tidy. You lost a fair amount of blood, Inspector Piasecki."

"Natalie…"

"Ms. Fletcher's being tended to. Now let me do my job, will you?" She stopped what she was doing and eyed him again. "If you keep shoving at me, mister, I'm going to sedate you. My job was a lot easier when you were out cold."

"How long?" he managed to croak.

"Not long enough." She knotted the suture, and snipped. "We picked the glass out of your shoulder. Not much damage there, but this arm's nasty. Fifteen stitches." She granted him a smile. "Some of my best work."

"I want to see Natalie." His voice was raspy, but there was no mistaking the threat underneath. "Now."

"Well, you can't. You're going to stay where I put you until I'm done. Then, if you're a very good boy, I'll have someone check on Ms. Fletcher for you."

Ry used his good arm and grabbed the doctor by the coat. "Now."

She only sighed. In his condition, she was well aware, she could knock him back with a shrug. But agitation wasn't going to help him. "Stay," she ordered, and went to the curtain. Pushing it aside, she called for a nurse. After a few brisk instructions, she turned back to Ry. "Your update's on the way. I'm Dr. Milano, and I'll be saving your life this evening."

"She was breathing," he said, as if daring Milano to disagree.

"Yes." She moved back to take his hand. "You took in a lot of smoke, Inspector. I'm going to treat you, and you're going to cooperate. After we've cleaned you out, I'll arrange for you to see Ms. Fletcher."

The nurse came back to the curtained opening, and Milano moved off again to hold a murmured consultation with her.

"Smoke inhalation," she announced. "And she's in shock. A few minor burns and lacerations. I imagine we'll keep her in our fine establishment for a day or two." Her face softened when she saw Ry's eyes close in relief. "Come on, big guy, let's work together here."

He might be weak as a baby, but he wasn't going to let them shove him into a hospital room. Over Milano's disgusted protests, he walked out into the waiting area. Deirdre sprang up from a chair the moment she saw him.

"Natalie?"

"They're working on her. They told me she's going to be all right."

"Thank God." With a muffled sob, Deirdre covered her face.

"Now, Ms. Marks, why don't you tell me what

the hell you were doing outside the office tonight?"

Taking a deep breath, Deirdre levered herself
into a chair. "I'd be glad to. I called Natalie's
brother," she added. "I suppose he's already on his
way out. I told him she was hurt, but I tried to play
it down."

Ry merely nodded. Though he hated the weakness, he had to sit. Nausea was threatening again.
"That was probably wise."

"I also gave him the bare bones of what I found
out earlier today." She took a long breath. "I
haven't been in the office the last couple of days—
I've been nursing a cold. But I took work home.
Including files and a couple of computer disks
Natalie gave me before she went on the road. I was
running figures, and I found some discrepancies.
Some very large discrepancies. The kind that
equals embezzlement."

Money, Ry thought. It almost always came
around to money. "Who?"

"I can't say for sure—"

He interrupted her, in a tone that made her
shiver. "Who?"

"I'm telling you, I can't be sure. I can only narrow it down, considering how and where the

money was siphoned off. And I'm not giving you a name so you can go off and beat somebody to a pulp."

Which was exactly what he had in mind, she was certain. Despite the fact that he looked like a survivor of a quick trip to hell, there was murder in his eyes.

"I could be wrong. I need to talk to Natalie," she said, half to herself. "As soon as I was sure of what I'd found, I tried to contact her in Colorado, but she'd already left. I knew she'd go by the office before heading home. It's the way she works. So I decided I'd meet her there. Tell her what I'd found out." She tapped the briefcase at her feet. "Show her. When I parked outside, I glanced up. I saw—"

She shut her eyes, knew she would relive it over and over again. "I saw these crazy lights in some of the windows. At first I didn't know, then I realized what it was. I called 911 on the car phone." Unnerved by the memory, she pressed a hand to her mouth. "I ran inside, told the security guard. And we heard, like, an explosion."

She was crying now, quietly. "I knew she was up there. I just knew it. But I didn't know what to do."

"Yes, you did. And you did it." Ry patted her awkwardly on the shoulder.

"Inspector?" Milano strode out, the usual scowl on her face. "I got you a pass to see your lady, not that you'll bother to thank me for it."

He was on his feet. "She's okay?"

"She's stabilized, and sedated. But you can look at her, since that seems to be your goal in life."

He glanced back at Deirdre. "Are you going to wait?"

"Yes. If you'd just let me know how she is."

"I'll be back." He headed off after the quick-stepping doctor.

Natalie's room was private, and dimly lit. She lay very still, very pale. But her hand, when he took it in his, was warm.

"Are you planning on spending the night here?" Milano asked from the doorway.

"Are you going to give me a hard time about it?" Ry returned without looking around.

"Who, me? I aim to serve. It's not likely she'll wake up, but that's not going to stop you. Neither is trying to sleep in that hideously uncomfortable chair.

"I'm a fireman, Doc. I can sleep anywhere."

"Well, fireman, make yourself at home. I'll go tell your friend in the waiting room that all's well."

"Yeah." He never took his eyes from Natalie's face. "That'd be good."

"Oh, you're more than welcome," Milano said sourly, and closed the door behind her.

Ry pulled the chair up to the side of the bed and sat with Natalie's hand in his.

He dozed once or twice. Occasionally a nurse came into the room and scooted him out. It was during one of those short, restless breaks that he saw Boyd rushing down the corridor.

"Piasecki."

"Captain. She's sleeping." Ry gestured toward the door. "There."

Without another word, Boyd moved past him and inside.

Ry walked into the waiting lounge, poured a cup of muddy coffee, and stared out the window. He couldn't think. It seemed better that way, just to let the night drift. If he focused, he would see it again, the terror on her face, the fire around her. And he would remember how he'd felt, carrying her down flight after flight, not knowing if she was alive or dead.

The burning on his hand made him look down. He saw he'd crushed the paper cup into a ball and spilled the hot coffee over his bandaged hands.

"Want another?" Boyd said from behind him.

"No." Ry tossed the cup away, and wiped his hand on his jeans. "You want to go outside and pound on me awhile?"

With a short laugh, Boyd poured coffee for himself. "Have you taken a look in a mirror?"

"Why?"

"You look like hell." Experimentally, Boyd sipped. It was even more pathetic than precinct coffee. "Worse than hell. It wouldn't look good for me to start swinging at a guy in your condition."

"I heal quick." When Boyd said nothing, Ry shoved his hands in his pockets. "I told you I wouldn't let her get hurt. I damn near killed her."

"You did?"

"I lost it. I knew it wasn't just Clarence. I knew there was somebody behind it. But I was so...wrapped up in her. I never thought about him getting another torch, or trying something himself. The phones, damn it. I heard the phones ringing."

Intrigued, Boyd sat back. "Which means?"

"A delaying device," Ry shot back, whirling around. "It's a classic. Matchsticks, soaked in accelerant. Tape them to the phone, call the number. The phone rings, the ringer sparks the match."

"Clever. But you know, you can't think of everything all the time."

"It's my job to think of everything."

"And to have a crystal ball."

His voice was raw from the abuse his throat had taken, tight with the emotion he couldn't afford to let loose. "I was supposed to take care of her."

"Yeah." Acknowledging that, Boyd sipped again. "I made a lot of calls on the flight from Denver. One of the perks of Fletcher Industries is having a private plane at your disposal. I talked to the fire marshal, to the doctor who treated Natalie, to Deirdre Marks. You got her out, carried her down every damn step in that building. How many stitches have you got in that arm?"

"That's hardly the point."

"The point is, the fire marshal gave me some idea of what you were facing up there on the forty-second floor, and what kind of shape you were in when you got her outside. Her doctor told me that if she'd been in there another ten minutes, it isn't likely she'd be sleeping right now. So, do I want to punch you? I don't think so. I owe you my sister's life."

Ry remembered how she had looked when he laid her on the ground next to the engine. How she looked now, pale and still, in a hospital bed. "You don't owe me anything."

"Natalie's as important to me as she is to you." Boyd set his coffee aside and rose. "What did you do to tick her off?"

Ry grimaced. "We're working it out."

"Well, good luck." Boyd held out a hand.

After a moment, Ry clasped it with his. "Thanks."

"I figure you're going to be here awhile. I've got a little job to do."

Ry tightened his grip, and narrowed his eyes. "Deirdre told you who's responsible."

"That's right. I also spoke with my counterpart here in Urbana while I was in the air. It's being taken care of." He saw the look in Ry's eyes, understood it. "This part's up to my team, Ry. You and yours just make damn sure you hang him for the arson."

"Who?" Ry said between his teeth.

"Donald Hawthorne. I got it down to four likely suspects two days ago." He smiled a little. "Some background checks, bank and phone records. Sometimes it pays to be a cop."

"And you didn't pass the information along to me."

"I intended to, when I narrowed it down a bit further. Now I have, and I am."

Boyd knew what it was to love, to need to protect, and to live with the terror of seeing your woman fight for her life.

"Listen," he said briskly, "if you kill him—however much it might appeal to both of us right now—I'd have to arrest you. I'd hate to throw my brother-in-law in a cell."

Ry unfisted his hands long enough to stick them in his pockets. "I'm not your brother-in-law."

"Not yet. Go on in with her, get some sleep."

"You'd better put Hawthorne somewhere where I can't find him."

"I intend to," Boyd said as he walked away.

Natalie stirred at dawn. Ry was watching the way the slats of light through the blinds bloomed over her when her lashes fluttered.

He bent over her, talking softly, quickly, so that her first clear thoughts wouldn't be fearful ones. "Natalie, you're okay. We got out okay. You just swallowed some smoke. Everything's all right now. You've been sleeping. I'm right here. I don't want you to talk. Your throat's going to be miserable for a while."

"You're talking," she whispered, her eyes still closed.

"Yeah." And it felt as though he'd swallowed a

flaming sword. "That's why I don't recommend it."

She swallowed and winced. "We didn't die."

"Doesn't look like it." Gently he cupped her head and held a cup of water so that she could sip through the straw. "Just take it easy."

There was a fear lurking deep inside her. But she had to know. "Are we burned badly?"

"We're not burned. A couple of singes, maybe."

Relief made her shiver. "I can't feel anything, except—" She reached up to touch the bruise on her forehead.

"Sorry." He pressed his lips to the lump, felt himself begin to tremble, and drew back again. "You got that when I tackled you."

She opened her eyes then. They felt weighted. Her whole body felt weighted. "Hospital?" she asked. Then her breath caught as she focused on him. Scratches on his face, a bandage at his temple, and a larger one that started just below his shoulder and nearly reached the elbow. His hands, his beautiful hands, were wrapped in gauze.

"Oh, God, Ry. You're hurt."

"Cuts and bruises." He smiled at her. "Singed my hair a little."

"You need a doctor."

"I've had one, thanks. I don't think she likes me. Now shut up and rest."

"What happened?"

"You're going to have to move your office." When she started to speak again, he held up a hand. "I'll tell you what I know if you keep quiet. Otherwise, I'll just leave you to stew. Deal?" Satisfied, he sat on the edge of the bed. "Deirdre tried to call you in Colorado," he began.

When he finished, her head was throbbing. Impotent fury ate away at the remnant of the sedative until she was wide awake and aching. Anticipating her, Ry laid his hand over her mouth.

"There's nothing you can do until you're on your feet. Not much you can do then. It's up to the departments—fire and police. And it's being handled. Now I'm going to ring for the nurse so they can take a look at you."

"I don't—" Her protest turned into a spasm of coughing. By the time she'd regained control, a nurse was gesturing Ry out of the room.

She didn't see him again for more than twenty-four hours.

"You could use another day here, Nat." Boyd crossed his feet at the ankles as he watched

Natalie pack the small overnight case he'd brought her.

"I hate hospitals."

"You've made that clear. I need your word you're taking a full week off, at home, or I'm calling in the troops. And not just Cilla, but Mom and Dad."

"There's no need for them to fly all the way out here."

"That's up to you, pal."

She pouted. "Three days off."

"A full week. Anything less is a deal-breaker. I can be just as tough a negotiator as you," he said with a grin. "It's in the blood."

"Fine, fine, a week. What difference does it make?" She snatched up the water glass and drank. It seemed she could never get enough to drink these days. "Everything's in shambles. Half my building's destroyed, one of my most trusted executives is responsible. I don't even have an office to go to."

"You'll take care of that. Next week. Hawthorne has a lot to answer for. The fact that he didn't know you and Ry were in the building isn't going to save him."

"All for greed." Too angry to pack the few

things Boyd had brought her, she paced. Her body still felt weak, but there was too much energy boiling within to allow her to keep still. "Draining a little here, a little there, losing it on speculative stocks. Then draining more and more, until he was so desperate he risked burning down entire buildings just to destroy records and delay the audit records."

She whirled back. "How frustrated he must have been when I told him I had duplicates of everything that was lost in the warehouse fire."

"And he wasn't sure where you kept them. Fire destroys everything," Boyd pointed out. "So, he'd take one of the buildings, and hope. If he didn't hit, the confusion in the aftermath would keep everyone so busy, you wouldn't get around to the audit until, he hoped, he'd managed to replace the siphoned funds."

"So he thought."

"He doesn't know you like I do. You always get things done on time. The office was his last shot, and the most desperate, since he had to do it himself. When we picked him up and he found out you and Ry had been in there and that he was facing attempted murder charges, he gave us everything."

"I trusted him," Natalie murmured. "I can't stand

knowing I could be so wrong about anyone I thought I knew." She glanced up as the door opened.

"Good to see you, Ry," Boyd said, and rose. This looked like his cue to make a quick and discreet exit.

Ry nodded at Boyd, then focused on Natalie. "Why aren't you in bed?"

"I've been discharged."

"You're not ready to leave the hospital."

"Excuse me." Boyd slipped toward the door. "I have a sudden urge for a cup of bad coffee."

Neither Natalie nor Ry bothered to say good-bye. They only continued to argue in raspy croaks.

"Do you have a medical degree now, Inspector?"

"I know what shape you were in when you got here."

"Well, if you'd bothered to check in since, you'd have seen that I'm recovered."

"I had a lot of details to tie up," he told her. "And you needed to rest."

"I'd rather have had you."

He held out the flowers. "I'm here now."

She sighed. Should she let him off the hook so easily when she'd been pining for him for so long? And why shouldn't she make him pay a bit for dumping her for the most ridiculous reason?

"Why don't you go take those daffodils to someone who needs them."

He tossed them on the bed. "I'm going to go talk to the doctor."

"You certainly will not talk to *my* doctor. I don't need your permission to leave the hospital. You didn't ask me for mine. And I did not need rest. I needed to see you. I was worried about you."

"Were you?" Encouraged, he lifted a hand to her face.

"I wanted you here, Ry. Dozens of other people came, but obviously you didn't see the need—"

"I had work," he shot back. "I wanted to get the evidence on that sonofabitch as soon as possible. It's all I can do. I'd kill him if I could get to him."

She started to snap back, then felt an icy chill at the look on his face. "Stop that." Unnerved, she turned her back on him, away from the murder in his eyes, and tossed a robe in her case. "I don't want to hear you talk that way."

"I didn't know if you were alive." He spun her around, his fingers digging into her shoulders. "I didn't know. You weren't moving. I didn't know if you were breathing." Suddenly he dragged her against him and buried his face in her hair. "God, Natalie, I've never been so scared."

"All right." She brought her arms around him, to soothe. "Don't think about it."

"I didn't let myself, until you woke up yesterday. Since then I haven't been able to think about anything else." Struggling for composure, he eased away. "I'm sorry."

"Sorry for saving my life? For risking your own to keep me from being hurt? You shielded me from the explosion. You carried me through fire." She shook her head quickly, before he could speak. "Don't tell me you were doing your job. I don't give a damn whether you want to be a hero or not. You're mine."

"I love you, Natalie."

Her heart softened and swelled. Carefully she turned and picked up the daffodils. It was foolish to waste their emotions on anger. They were alive. "You mentioned that, before we were interrupted."

"There's something else I should have mentioned. Why I pushed you away."

Staring down, she flicked a finger over a bright yellow trumpet. "You listed the reasons."

"I listed the excuses. Not the reason. Maybe you could look at me while I grovel?"

She turned back, trying to smile. "It's not necessary, Ry."

"Yeah, it is. You haven't decided whether you're going to give me another chance yet." He reached out, tucked her hair behind her ear. "I could wear you down eventually, because you're crazy about me. But you deserve to know what was going on in my head."

She stiffened automatically. "I don't think arrogance is very appropriate, so why don't you—"

"I was scared," he said quietly, and watched the heat fade from her eyes. "Of you, of me. Of us." He let out a long breath when she said nothing. "I didn't think I could say it. Admit it. Not until I realized what it was to be *really* scared. Down-to-the-bone scared. It makes being afraid of being in love pretty stupid."

"Then it looks like we were both stupid, because I was scared, too." Her mouth curved a little. "You were more stupid, of course."

"My whole life," he said quietly, "I've never felt anything like what I feel for you. Not for anyone."

"I know." Her breath trembled out. "I know. It's the same with me."

"And it just keeps getting bigger, and scarier. Are you going to give me another chance?"

She looked at him—the bony face, the dark eyes, the unruly hair. "I probably owe you that much, seeing as you've saved my life and come clean, groveled and apologized." Her smile spread. "I suppose I could give us both another chance."

"Want to marry me?"

The flowers drifted to the floor as her fingers went numb. "Excuse me?"

"With you feeling generous, it seemed like a good time to push my luck." Feeling foolish, he bent down and gathered up the daffodils. "But it can wait."

She cleared her aching throat, accepting the flowers again. "Would you mind repeating the question?"

His eyes shot back to hers. It took him a moment to find his voice again. It was a risk, he realized. One of the biggest risks he'd ever faced. And he had to leave his fate in her hands.

"Will you marry me?"

"I could do that," she said, and let out the breath she'd been holding, even as Ry let out his own. "Yes, I could do that." Laughing, she launched herself into his arms.

"I've got you." Dazzled, Ry buried his face in her hair. "I've got you, Legs, from now on." And kissed her.

"I want babies," she told him the minute her mouth was free.

"No kidding?" With a grin, he pushed her hair back so that he could read her face. What he saw made his heart leap. "Me, too."

"That makes it handy."

He scooped his arms under her legs and lifted her. "What do you say we get out of here and get started?"

She managed to snag her overnight case before he headed to the door. "That'll make it nine months from today." She kissed his cheek as he carried her from the room. "And I'm always on time."

In this case, she managed to be eight days early.

Ryan and Natalie Piasecki
are pleased to announce the birth of their son,
Fletcher Joseph Piasecki,
who arrived promptly at 4:45 a.m., January 5.
Fletcher weighted 7 pounds 10 ounces and has
ten fingers and ten toes.
Both parents counted.

Danger walks in the darkness...

Don't miss the next instalment of

NIGHT TALES

Night Shield
by
Nora Roberts

Coming next month!

"I killed a woman tonight.
One shot through the heart."

Undercover as a waitress, Detective Allison Fletcher is on the case that will make her career – breaking an organised gang of robbers. Then, at the scene of one of the burglaries, she has no choice but to shoot the woman holding a gun on her.

The robber's psychotic, controlling brother knows who killed his beloved sister, and he's out for revenge. When he breaks into Allison's flat, writing blood-red words on the walls, Allison knows she's in terrible danger. And her cop's shield won't be enough to protect her from a madman...

Read on for a preview!

NIGHT SHIELD

He didn't like cops.

His attitude had deep roots, and stemmed from spending his formative years dodging them, outrunning them – usually – or being hassled by them when his feet weren't fast enough. He'd picked his share of pockets by the time he'd turned twelve and knew the best, and most lucrative channels for turning a hot watch into cold cash.

He'd learned back then that knowing what time it was couldn't buy happiness, but the twenty bucks the watch brought in paid for a nice slice of the happiness pie. And twenty bucks cannily wagered swelled into sixty at three-to-one.

The same year he'd turned twelve, he'd invested his carefully hoarded takes and winnings in a small gambling enterprise that centered around point spreads and indulged his interest in sports.

He was a businessman at heart.

He hadn't run with gangs. First of all he'd never had the urge to join groups, and more importantly he didn't care for the pecking order such organisations required. Someone had to be in charge – and he preferred it to be himself.

Some people might say Jonah Blackhawk had a problem with authority.

They would be right.

He supposed the tide had turned right after he'd turned thirteen. His gambling interests had grown nicely – a little too nicely to suit certain more established syndicates.

He'd been warned off in the accepted way – he'd had the hell beat out of him. Jonah acknowledged the bruised kidneys, split lip and blackened eyes as a business risk. But before he could make his decision to move territories or dig in, he'd been busted. And busted solid.

Cops were a great deal more of an annoyance than business rivals.

But the cop who'd hauled his arrogant butt in had been different. Jonah had never pinned down what exactly separated this cop from the others in the line of shields and rule books. So, instead of being tossed into juvie – to which he was no stranger – he'd found himself yanked into programs, youth centers, counseling.

Oh, he'd squirmed and snapped in his own cold-blooded way, but this cop had a grip like a bear trap and hadn't let go. The sheer tenacity had been a shock. No one had held onto him before. Jonah had found himself rehabilitated almost despite himself, at least enough to see there were certain advantages to, if not working in the system, at least working the system.

Now, at thirty, no one would call him a pillar of Denver's community, but he was a legitimate businessman whose enterprises turned a solid profit and allowed him a lifestyle the hustling street kid couldn't have dreamed of.

He owed the cop, and he always paid his debts.

Otherwise, he'd have chosen to be chained naked and honey-smeared to a hill of fire ants rather than sit tamely in the outer office of the commissioner of police of Denver.

Even if the commissioner was Boyd Fletcher.

Passion. Power. Suspense.
It's time to fall under the spell of Nora Roberts.

From No. 1 *New York Times* bestselling author Nora Roberts

Nightshade
When a teenager gets caught up in making sadistic violent films, Colt Nightshade and Lieutenant Althea Grayson must find her before she winds up dead...

Night Smoke
When Natalie Fletcher's office is set ablaze, she must find out who wants her ruined – before someone is killed...

Night Shield
When a revengeful robber leaves blood-stained words on Detective Allison Fletcher's walls, she knows her cop's shield won't be enough to protect her...

**Passion. Power. Suspense.
It's time to fall under the spell of Nora Roberts.**